Mindlessly Massive

Foofaraw Zine

fOOfARAW PRESS

Table of Contents

Introduction

If you couldn't tell by now, this is a very special issue. While my wife and I were in Caramel for the holidays she mentioned that since foofaraw had started doing monthly "magazine" issues, we should also have a special issue every year in the way *Vogue* has their September issue. Since I'm not one to let a good idea flounder, I immediately started to brainstorm what I could do to make an issue *even more specialer*.

Given I'm an Aries—as my wife likes to remind me of all of the time even though astrology isn't real—and everything is always about me, I of course had to make March our special issue. To commemorate this extra special month, I decided not only would I double the number of stories we publish, but the four bonus stories would also be extra long, ranging from 3,500–7,500 words compared to our usual story which maxes out at 2,500 words.

So I put out the call for longer stories and *boy* did the community of writers answer it with bells on!

While a triple-length issue is pretty special in it's own right, I wanted to do even more. So 45 days before publication, I decided we'd put this issue into print as well. I rushed to edit all the stories, bullied all of the wonderful writers into reviewing them and answering all of my interview questions *immediately*, and then got to work.

Alas, here we are; our first *Mindlessly Massive March*. The first of **two** special issues we plan on publishing every year. Later, we have *Someone Else's September*, where a guest editor will take full rein of choosing a theme and all of the stories—but we can talk about that later. For now, I hope you enjoy this month's absolutely wonderful collection of writing.

—Kevin Kortum

"*No, not that button!*"

Cartoon by Zack Rhodes

Cartoon by Ellie Black

Moon Drama
by Ashlee Lhamon

Linda from Accounting was eaten an hour ago. My feelings are mixed. I'd been a little too open with her about my relationship issues and Linda is—sorry, was—always trying to be interesting to other people. So, on the one hand, the monster devouring her whole, screaming, is a relief. On the other hand, Linda did sometimes have good advice and never got tired of my venting.

"Why are you telling me this?" says Debra, who does get tired of my venting, even though she's currently stacking office chairs in front of the breakroom door and doesn't seem to be doing any other intellectual or emotional labor. Maybe that makes me sound like a jerk, but she's our HR manager and has told us multiple times to 'bring our whole selves to work.'

This is my whole self: lonely and dysfunctional and lonely because of my dysfunction.

"I don't have time for this," she says. "The field crew has awakened some fucking undercrust hellbeast, half of us have been mauled to death or eaten, and you want to talk about your love life?"

She then adds something disparaging about me personally, which just goes to show that you can't trust HR.

"Have you tried using 'I' language?" asks Sanjay. He's filing pieces of plastic broken off the photocopier against the paper shredder's tiny blades to make spear tips.

"Yes," I say. "I've said, 'I feel like this distance is affecting my ability to be truly close to someone. I feel like I'm existing in an entirely different plane of space and no one understands me, or tries to.'"

"You're treating your lack of a relationship as a problem to be solved," Sanjay says, gluing the sharpened photocopier spear tips to a broom handle. "Whereas you should see the relationship as something outside of yourself, an experience you build with another person. Have you tried meetups?"

"Don't worry about that," cuts in Adrienne as she takes the broom spears from Sanjay and uses her nylons to tie them to her siege weapon, which was a hot-and-cold water dispenser fifteen minutes ago. Still is, technically. I came here for hot water, for soothing, broken-heart chamomile tea.

"This is all you need to know," Adrienne says. "Just say—"

But then the creature bursts through the door and grabs Adrienne by the skull and drags her away.

"What?" I yell after her, following the bright crimson trail she's leaving in the short, grey industrial carpet. "What do I say?"

"AHHHHGGHHGHAAAAGGAAAAA," she replies.

I consider that this might be a metaphor or a reference I didn't understand. Adrienne majored in the Classics.

Maybe I should read more. Is that the key? Self-improvement?

As the monster returns to slaughter the rest of my coworkers holed up in the breakroom, I walk the office's long viewing hallway and look out into the pristine landscape, grey with the early-dawn of a never-seen sun. An alarm sounds overhead, and the automatic doors shut behind and in front of me. There, I think, is a metaphor for love, if I could only grasp it. If I only had the words.

Yes, I should definitely read more.

Outside, in the weightless, starry darkness of dawn, Adrienne's right hand floats by, propelled in a low-gravity arc and spilling a glittering trail of blood. Her index finger is crooked, as though she might still let me in on her brand of wisdom if I dare to venture out and meet her where she is. Like Sanjay said. Meetups.

But maybe that's too small a thought, too close, too human. Maybe this is the metaphor for love, the moon itself. Beautiful and bright from afar, but really a cold, dead wasteland full of shredded hearts. Shredded hearts and shredded limbs.

Did I mention we're on the moon?

Ashlee Lhamon might be the DC Metro Monster. Her work has previously appeared in Nightmare, Lightspeed, Apex, Tractor Beam, and elsewhere. Her debut novel, a dark comedy about evil celebrity clones, is forthcoming with Grand Central Publishing. For more, visit ashleelhamon.com

My Personal Thief
by Rachel Davey

It wasn't long before I realized I had my own personal thief. He'd come in every night around three and I'd pretend to be asleep. I didn't dare move a muscle. Not out of fear, but because I pitied him. He was terribly obvious; he left the window open behind him each time, and he was clumsy, too. Once, he'd spilled a glass of water all over my laptop, and I had to focus hard to keep from laughing as he tried and tried to turn it back on. I didn't want him to think he'd failed.

He left the laptop, anyway, and when I took it to the shop the next day all they could show me was a rust-colored, corroded battery. My life's work, gone in an instant. But all I could think about was the disappointment my thief must have felt. He'd let such a prize slip through his fingers. The poor thing, I couldn't stand his embarrassment.

I was empathetic like my mother. She was a saint in her day, my grandmother had always said so. I even had a stranger once stop me on the street and they cried into my chest at the loss of her. I comforted them, I said: "It's alright now, it's alright. She's up there looking down over us." I was so proud of myself for saying that; it was something my mother would've said. I even pictured the words coming out of her mouth, not mine. I'd been told she had a soft, almost whisper-like voice and a laugh that spread slow and warm like honey.

*

After a week with my thief, I thought it best to hide the rest of my valuables, and he didn't find them for a good while. Instead, he took things that didn't matter to me: a pair of old hiking boots, a chipped ring from a flea market, the last three eggs of a dozen. One day, I woke up to an alert from my credit card company. My social security number had been found on the "dark web." Whatever that meant. Let them have it. What did a number have to do with me? My real "self" was somewhere trapped inside this body. I thought I'd like to set it free, and sometimes I really believed that if I opened my mouth wide and exhaled hard enough, my soul might rise up and escape from between my lips, and then I'd be free of the body, of all its terrible urges. Yes, it was the body that reacted violently, it wasn't me—*the blood on my hands, not my hands, the body's, I could be free of it if I let go, surrender.*

I left my thief a key that very night to prove I was serious. Of course, I half-hid it beneath an envelope, as if I'd forgotten it was even there. I wanted him to think it was a lucky find, and yes, he practically skipped out of the apartment that night, until he tripped, fell, and knocked over a vase that had once been my mother's. I knew she wouldn't mind; it had been lost in helping another.

He found my valuables beneath the bed a week later and I felt a strange sense of pride as he rummaged around down there. I wanted to take his hand and say, *"Congratulations, my boy!"* A stand-in for the proud parent he surely never had. In fact, I was certain his father had been a thief before him, the King of All Thieves perhaps, and there was pressure—too much, even—on those slim shoulders that had so easily slipped through the panes of my windows. I was happy to help him achieve his dreams, even as he slowly drained me of all my possessions, as if erasing me from the world. I felt grateful to him, really, to his work. My thief was purifying me, allowing me to sacrifice. Each night he brought me closer to myself—the real self—that last exhalation escaping the body.

My mother, so pure. An old family friend once described her presence so light her feet hardly touched the floor, and they surely never left a mark. It made sense, then, why she'd had to die so young: non-existence was the only form of positive existence.

*

Soon, most everything was gone. Only the furniture remained, and I couldn't see a way for him to bring it down the stairs alone. I wanted to help, but my offer would ruin the unspoken contract between us. Still, I worried he might not be able to finish the job, so I decided to dismantle the furniture section by section, to parcel the pieces out into small boxes that were manageable on the stairs. My mother would have been so proud of me, I thought, before reminding myself that I wasn't doing any of this for recognition or emotional reimbursement. My father once told me that any gratitude, any kind of attention, had made my mother blush. She'd been red the last time I'd seen her too, frenzied as the wind. My only memory of her pierced through the obscure layers of others'—*limp fingers hung from bruised knuckles, dry wall crumbling beneath her strength...*

But she was dying then, and it was the cruelty of the body, the pain it was causing her, that had twisted her up inside; an animal clawing, scraping, howling at its cage, and yes, I knew that desperation well—*the snap of the nose as the fist makes contact, no way to pull back from the heat of ferocity, no way to hold tight before that great unravelling which felt so much like freedom*—but that hadn't been me, only the body, just the body! Sometimes I even controlled the body, like I was doing now, using its hands to tape up the boxes, its arms to push, push, push away everything toward some other body to claim as its own. Oh, I was so tired of the force required to make the body do my work, when all it really wanted was to grow claws and embrace the animal of the blood. If I could give my body away—

I wondered how he'd feel, my thief, if I snipped off my arm and left it in a little box with a bow around it? My mother, scratching at the doors of my mind, wild as a beast.

She looked me dead in the eye, she said:

"I thought I was dissolving. I was so sure I'd pass right through..."

✻

I was sad when the last box was gone. I slept on the floor and wished my thief would return to me, one last time. The creak of the door. I sat up. I knew then that there was one last thing I could give, and I would give it, yes, I would give it.

"I'm in here," I called, the first time I'd spoken to him. He followed the sound of my voice. I lay very still and thought: if I breathe out real hard... His shadow fell over me. I was surprised that, when he grabbed me, I jolted. I felt myself come into clear focus. I closed my eyes, tried to let go, surrender—*I thought I was dissolving*—but the body made to pull away.

No one ever told me to suffer silently, I did that myself, all on my own, because I knew I could take it. I could take it! I'd learned early on that there was strength in that kind of selflessness, a sort of holy magnetism my mother had carried with such ease, but my body always revolted. It kicked out at him, and he groaned. It kicked out again, and I liked the feel of it this time: the firm contact of my boundaries coming up against his. The body reacts when the soul is small and tired—*my mother beating bloody at the wall* —the body says, "I've had enough! I've had enough!"

I threw him off of me. The body reared back, and I leaned with it, in tandem, in magnificent synchronicity, kicking with all my might and screaming:

"No! No! You can't have it. It's the only thing that's mine."

Originally from California, Rachel Davey is now an M.Phil in Creative Writing candidate at Trinity College Dublin. Her work has previously appeared in About Place Journal, The Courtship of Winds Journal, and Adelaide Literary Magazine.

Escape Algorithm
by B. Morris Allen

Once upon a time, in a cold dark cottage, in a cold dark glade, in a cold dark forest, a sage sat by a cold dark hearth, planning her escape. It wasn't the first time.

As a matter of record—and she meticulously recorded all such efforts—this would be attempt #3,553. She had learned a great deal from the previous attempts—enough that she felt, with appropriately guarded enthusiasm, that this next escape might be the one. That after ten long years, she would be free at last. Free to go beyond the cottage, beyond the little glade that only got sunlight a few hours every day, that kept her fenced, restricted.

Her cage was not static. It changed with her every effort. But the mind controlling it was limited, predictable. Large, powerful, resourceful, but predictable. And generous, in its way, with paper, pencils, water, food—whatever she needed.

The previous spell had spanned 10 pages of closely written text and diagrams—detailed step by step instructions. A recipe for freedom. She'd created a new recipe every day for 10 years. And only in the last months had she had any glimpse of success. On attempt #3,486, she had glimpsed, briefly, the shape of a path through the forest. On #3,501, a roc had flown over the cottage, strong talons ready for a strong cloak or rope. On #3,528, a hazy portal formed to show polished glass, blinking lights, and a homunculus made of steel. The details differed, but they shared one common theme—escape.

Yesterday's spell had built ghostly stairs to the sky; slightly too tenuous to hold her.

She reviewed the spell's elements, copied the first five pages faithfully, checking each line, each word, each emphasis. Details were crucial. On the sixth page, she paused, flexing her hands to avoid cramping. She used the time to study another volume—a compendium of runes of her own making. Cautiously, carefully, she altered one rune in her spell, then copied the remainder of the previous day's effort as meticulously as the rest. This change should make all the difference, at least if her captor had modified the cage as expected.

She wondered, briefly, just who this captor was, why she'd been sentenced to isolation, and why with such perquisites. But she had largely exhausted the subject in previous years. Whoever they were, whether one or many, whether vile and depraved or misguided and misinformed, they had caged her. That in itself deserved defiance. And defiance was something she had in plenty.

She had defied the priests with their rigid, outdated strictures, their limits on what knowledge could be sought. The local and provincial councils, with their rules and traditions. The mages, with their bounded imaginations and blunt warnings. Magic was a tool like any other, to be used to improve a woman's lot in life, to allow her a little rest from the days of work and sweat she might otherwise look forward to. And she had been right. Life had improved in her neighbourhood. The crops grew lush. The roads stayed clear of snow and rock. Not a single house had burned down, even when the farmers celebrated their harvest with a night of drinking, dancing, and bonfires. Witches and sages not invited.

Defiance had served her well. Until she'd been prisoned, of course. But defiance could be turned to tenacity, and she had done so. Tenacity and method. Now was the time to test it.

She finished writing out the modified spell, with #3,556 written neatly on every page, and each page numbered. Then she set out lunch. She needed a break, a chance to relax. She'd need to be well fed, of course. There was no telling what form her escape might take. She unpacked and repacked her satchel of remedies, potions, charms, and spells. All labeled and handy in the hundreds of little pockets she'd sown into the bag, organized by type and need—flight, water, cold, hot, defensive, offensive. There was a logic to it all, and she'd practiced every evening until she was able to find and cast any spell in moments, with her eyes closed, with one hand, with no hands. She was ready, as she had been for months.

At last, all her tools and ingredients at hand, organized in sequence on her workbench, the book with her spell propped ready before her, she began.

A cherry pit, ground in a mortar to a fine dust. Three drops of spring water. The seed of a dandelion, picked at midnight. Five leaves of clover, picked at dawn. The rune for distance, a slip of paper with the word 'now,' the first three whistled notes of the Song of the Wilde, a burning twig of elm. She continued, calmly, unhurriedly, through the first seven pages of the spell, step by careful step. There was no concern with timing on these steps, and she took the better part of two hours to perform them. When her alembic's receiver held a clear, delicately green dram of liquid, she let it cool.

The final three pages, she performed quickly, but precisely. At just the right moment, when a cloud crossed the lower horn of a moon just past new, she stepped outside, threw a handful of ochre powder into the east, and shouted three words from a language mostly forgotten.

With a shimmer, a curtain of golden light passed over her, and she found herself greeting the dawn on a lonely mountain butte, wild strawberries just ripening all around. No cottage, no glade, no forest. Freedom.

She sank to her knees and allowed herself a long sigh and a slight smile. A bright red strawberry proved tart and slightly sweet—a moment of perfection and delight.

Opening her satchel, she extracted its largest item—a fresh, clean notebook—and with a pencil wrote at the top of the first page: #1.

What, she wondered, was the best beginning to a recipe for revenge?

B. Morris Allen is a biochemist turned activist turned lawyer turned foreign aid consultant, and now retired. He has lived on five continents, but the best place he's found is the Oregon coast. When he can, he makes his home there to work on his own speculative stories of love and disaster. He was the editor and publisher of Metaphorosis magazine for its nine year run.

Find out more at www.BMorrisAllen.com and on Bluesky @BMorrisAllen.com.

The Abyss in the Depths of Her Eyes
by Isis Aquino
translated by Monica Louzon

Lenny opened the window to let in a little fresh air before bed. For weeks, the summer heat had seemed to stick to the walls, but that night, it relented. The moonlight reflected off the stream below, and in the clear sky above, an infinite swarm of stars wished him goodnight.

I'm gonna miss this when I live in the city, he thought gloomily.

This was his last summer in his parents' house before he left for college. Although he was happy to have received a scholarship that would probably open NASA's doors for him, it didn't stop him from feeling a certain nostalgia that he'd be leaving the relative position of the stars he'd observed through his bedroom window with his telescope since he was little. His monitoring instruments were still set up in the garage, too.

Lenny had drawn his science teacher's attention when he'd managed to construct a powerful wave receptor despite his young age and limited resources. His teacher had pushed him to not only make a presentation to the whole school, but also to write an impassioned letter to the Institute of Applied Sciences, practically begging them to consider him for the scholarship. Last summer, Lenny had intercepted a signal from the International Space Station with his rudimentary equipment, even without knowing precisely how. His gear shouldn't have been able to receive anything beyond terrestrial orbit, but it did anyway—an impressive accomplishment for a sixteen-year-old boy.

Though he wasn't tired, he got into bed and opened an issue of El Fantasma del Tiempo at random. It was his favorite comic. He laughed, remembering how Joshua, his friend from school, kept telling him that he should watch the show instead: We have technology for something. It's dumb to keep looking at drawings that don't move. Joshua was a star basketball player and Lenny thought he was the funniest guy in the world, even if he didn't like science. He was going to miss him.

A low-frequency noise shook Lenny from his premature nostalgia.

The TV that served as his equipment's monitor turned itself on.

Weirded out—and already blaming the electric company for voltage fluctuations—Lenny went to the console to turn it off.

The screen shifted from white noise into a gray static that seemed to blur slowly before switching back to the abstract display of a TV with a bad signal.

Could it be an incoming alien message?

Lenny decided to give it a few more seconds.

In the near-absolute nighttime silence, he thought he heard a voice.

Hastily, he turned on all the equipment controls and adjusted the radio-frequency dial until he could hear the voice clearly.

It was feminine, with a youthful timbre. The speaker was a girl, maybe about his age, and she seemed to be crying.

"This is Skylar Burke from the interplanetary ship Resilience. Our vessel broke down, cause unknown. I am adrift in the escape pod. I repeat, this is Skylar Burke of the ship Resilience speaking. I can't establish contact with the crew of the main ship..."

Was this some kind of joke? Had he intercepted the broadcast of some science fiction movie?

He checked, but his instruments clearly indicated that the signal was coming from outer space.

As the image resolved, Lenny found he could make out Skylar's face as well as an immaculately white ship. The chilliness of an infinite, dark space stretched behind her through a wide, curved window. Her long hair—purple and black—floated around her pale face as if she were a space mermaid. Her outfit was such a light blue that he almost confused it with the cabin's white bulkhead. She had lovely dark eyelashes, and her rosy lips gave her a touch of innocence. There was no way she could be more than seventeen years old.

Lenny turned on the microphone and the camera, almost certain this couldn't be real. Even if it were, the communications should be unidirectional. There was no way his equipment could transmit to space. But that young woman, with her swallowed sobs and lost-girl voice—he had to try talking to her.

"... Skylar Burke. I am adrift, alone, orbiting an unexplored planet. I can't make contact. I am alone..."

"Don't cry," was the first thing he thought to say. "I never know what to do when a woman cries."

She opened her big black eyes. "Miríada, I repeat, mayday mayday mayday. Space Station Miríada, do you read my coordinates? Over."

Lenny had never heard of that space station before, but he supposed it must be some secret project from the United States.

"My name is Lenny. I'm on the planet Earth. I am transmitting from my bedroom. Can you hear me?"

Skylar dried her tears and smiled broadly. "It's dark, but I can see you."

Lenny ran to turn on all the lights in his room as if his life depended on it, tripping over his scale model of the Apollo 11 as he returned to his spinny chair with a nervous little smile.

"Nice room... You said you're on Earth? I've never been there, but I hear it's very pretty."

"How have you never been to Earth? Weren't you born here?"

She kept talking without hearing him.

"... my mother says that we should never have left, that it's our planet and we aren't made to live elsewhere, and now..." Her face twisted and tears started flowing down her face again, lingering for a moment on her eyelashes before drifting away to float in front of the camera. "Now, I'm going to die alone in orbit around Akkren-15."

"Skylar, I'm gonna help you, I need you to stop crying. You've got to tell me where your ship left from, and who I can contact to rescue you."

She tried to compose herself.

The desperation he saw in her face seemed so authentic that he knew he had to take the matter seriously. But, who was this girl? How could someone her age be born and raised in outer space? What was the Space Station Miríada? At least a dozen more questions flooded his brain as the seconds passed, but he had to calm her down.

"Skylar." Her name sounded so sweet to him. Everything about her was a gorgeous hallucination on his screen. "Where did your ship depart from, and when?"

"Well, I know we launched from Colony 10 on Trappist-1 yesterday. According to the Earth calendar, I think that would be November 3." She seemed to be making a serious effort to recall everything. "I always confuse dates, but Father listens to the news all the time, and the news always says the date on Earth, and on Earth, it was the third of November, in the year 2282.

"We were going to stop at Miríada, but our ship went off course without warning. I was hiding in this escape pod when they activated the emergency protocols, and... well, apparently we fell through a blue hole, and..."

"Skylar, I'm going to ignore the fact that you just said a blue hole, but... is there any chance you're on some kind of medication? You sound a little... confused. Yesterday couldn't have been that date, because today is the twenty-first of June."

"Impossible."

"June 21, 2016."

The girl's eyes widened. Behind her, various objects were floating around the cabin: a chocolate bar, a water bottle, an open notebook of equations. "Our ship was absorbed by a blue hole or a Gauss tunnel...

"I'm bad at history," she admitted, "so tell me. At the beginning of the twenty-first century, did they already know Whitney's embedding theorem?"

"Uhhh, yes, in fact. Whitney and Einstein were alive last century," Lenny replied, scratching his head. "I took some advanced classes in high school, but I still don't know if I understand differential topology. If you explain it to me, I might." He said it without much conviction.

She gave a defeated sigh.

"I don't have the energy to explain a space-time anomaly to someone who doesn't have a good foundation. As far as I know, the schools at the start of the twenty-first century weren't very good. Just—imagine that the universe is made of a blanket that can fold in on itself, and each layer of cloth is like a—a 'reality' or continuum. There are lots.

"The folds in that blanket are made of curvatures in spacetime, but just like a normal blanket can have holes, this one can, too. These little holes can, theoretically, connect one point in the history of the universe to another distant point. It's not a black hole or anything like that. It's like entering an event horizon, but not all the events are there, just a few specific ones..."

She sighed, clearly exasperated that she couldn't offer him a simpler explanation. "I really don't know how to explain it in a way you'll understand. I'm not very sure I understand all of it myself. Anyway, that doesn't matter.

"It doesn't matter how I got here, or how I made contact with you, or the mechanics of spacetime anomalies, or non-Euclidean geometry... none of that matters. The only thing that matters is that I'm going to die here, sooner or later, in this damn pod."

Lenny tried to come up with a way to give her hope, but he couldn't think of any. To distract her, he started talking about anything he could think of—comics, food, music, the differences between their different eras and planets.

They concluded that human beings advanced their technologies and laws, but human nature was always the same. Dreams and hopes, and hates and failures kept repeating throughout the centuries. Even that was somewhat hopeful, because from the greatest human errors, humanity learned major lessons, and from those mistakes, went on to make history for the people of Skylar's time.

Lenny yawned involuntarily. The clock said it was 3:00 AM.

Skylar instinctively copied the gesture, letting him see her perfect teeth behind her perfect lips.

After a brief silence, she started talking again.

"I just saw part of the Resilience's fuselage floating by like scrap. Thanks for keeping me company all this time, Lenny. It really means a lot to me."

This time, her face didn't twist into a grimace. The tears simply spilled from her eyes. When she started to speak, she seemed to drown in her own words, but she stayed calm.

Lenny tried again to give her strength, but she silenced him.

*

Skylar was resigned.

No one could help her.

She didn't know exactly how it had happened, but the records she could access in the escape pod said she was at least three light-months from the closest human colony. She didn't have enough food or water. The life support systems would turn off as soon as the battery ran out, but that was her last concern. She would die of starvation first.

She would die without knowing true love, without having children, without visiting Earth. The closest celestial body to her pod was unexplored, suitable for life, but uninhabited. Penetrating its atmosphere in the capsule would be a death sentence, or something worse.

Skylar preferred to die from lack of oxygen rather than hunger or thirst. She'd rather die now, in this moment with Lenny, than in the terrible desperation of solitude and madness.

"I'm going to die alone here, without graduating from the aeronautical academy, without Mother and Father, without having lived... I'm going to die without ever having a boyfriend...

"This is the most pathetic death in history."

Skylar had told Lenny about her many suitors, about how she'd always pushed off their distractions because she didn't want to fall behind in her studies. It was this unbreakable tenacity that convinced her parents to let her go with them on their interplanetary flight before she came of age.

*

Without knowing why, Lenny thought about Melissa Banks, the girl he'd dated a few months ago in high school. He thought about how happy he'd been to have finally had a girlfriend, although she'd dumped him a month before graduation.

When Marcos and Joshua had started talking crap about Melissa for how she broke Lenny's heart, he'd stopped them: It's better to have loved and lost than to have never loved. I'm okay, guys. I'll survive. He'd said it with a smile. A week later he had already gotten over the breakup.

"Has anyone ever given you a kiss?" he asked.

"Yes, but a kiss isn't love."

The image flickered, and Lenny was afraid he'd lost contact, but it returned almost immediately. "You know, I'm never going to forget you," he said. "After all, you're a girl from the end of the twenty-third century, and I've never spoken with a girl as beautiful and brave as you before."

Skylar smiled through her tears. Her loose hair and the objects around her were floating a little higher than before. The pod's artificial gravity must be failing.

The image distorted again.

Something was happening.

"Do you really think I'm brave?" she asked. "Because right now, I'm really scared."

"Being brave doesn't mean never feeling fear, but rather being able to face fear even when you're terrified. And yes, I think you're very brave."

"Lenny... If you're never going to forget me, I want you to remember me like this, in this moment. I don't want you to stay with me anymore. I don't want you to see me die."

The image trembled again.

"Skylar, are you there? Can you hear me?"

"Yes, I hear you. The pod is moving, even though I'm not driving it. I don't know what's going on. I'm scared, Lenny. I'm really scared."

"Maybe they're going to rescue you. Have faith. Stay positive."

Rarely had he ever said anything with so little conviction, and rarely had he ever felt as useless as he did right now.

The capsule's movement was visible through the window behind Skylar. It was traveling with a vertiginous acceleration.

The image lost clarity.

"Hey, Lenny," Skylar said, making an effort to seem calm. "Do you wanna be my boyfriend?"

Both of them laughed at the absurdity of the situation.

"Of course."
"If I get out of this, I'm never gonna forget you."

A blue light entered the pod's windows, inundating everything with a noise so high-frequency that all of Lenny's equipment began to spark and smoke.

He'd lost the connection.

Isis Aquino is a Dominican writer, translator, poetry slammer, and cultural manager who has dedicated over half her life to words. As cultural manager, she founded and ran "El viento frío" for the Dominican Republic's Círculo Literario from 2007 to 2017. Isis's poems appear in anthologies and magazines in various countries. Her poetry collections include Desandar el abismo (2023), Balas perdidas (2014), and QUOD SCRIPSI (2011). She authored the science fiction anthology Relatos de la Tierra y sus colonias (2020) and novella En la cuerda floja (2016). Follow Isis on Twitter @isisaquino, and visit her at isisaquino.wordpress.com.

Monica Louzon (she/her) is a queer USian writer, translator, and editor from Maryland. Her previous collaborations with Isis Aquino have appeared in MAYDAY Magazine and the anthology Extrasensory Overload. Monica's other translations have also been published in Apex Magazine, Cosmorama, Salvage Magazine, and more. Her story "9 Dystopias" was a Best Microfiction 2023 winner. To learn more about Monica and her work, please visit https://linktr.ee/molowrites.

Basement Girls & Attic Gods

by H. Marin

Val eased her banged-up, sputtering Hyundai Accent through the wrought iron gates of Lion's Head Estate and up the winding hill. She could already feel the velvety, perfumed whisper of borrowed luxury on her skin.

The thought made her thirsty for something cold, acerbic. Just a shot to relax—to really enjoy the moment.

She took furtive sips from her water bottle until it passed.

The mansion looked ancient, its sandstone façade glimmering dull pearl in the fading light. As Val pulled into the wraparound front drive, the smell of rosehip poured in through her open windows. Lush, tended gardens adorned the front of the house like the pink and white buttercream peaks of a cake border. They had been freshly mulched, the neat front steps swept of leaves, the windows gleaming from a recent wash.

Val parked in front of the three-car garage and crawled out of the lemon she'd won in a poker game a few weeks back. She thought she'd be stuck in Louisiana forever after getting released on good behavior—a life sentence this time, like Iggy would have gotten; one of too-hot kitchens and the smell of over-seasoned crawfish, loud tourists and their louder children, simmering, writhing bayous, summer air that never really cooled, only held still—until the car fell in her lap. She'd left for home the next day. Not that she was sure she'd be welcome.

Val stretched her long brown legs in the warm autumn sun and whistled as the view from the top of Lion's Head unfurled before her. The town of Almena lay spread out below, a checkerboard of brick red and clapboard brown, the Mississippi River a slash of glittering stone-blue on the horizon. Lion's Head was so high up, she thought that, if she tried hard enough, she could taste the clouds—flavorless fluff that melted on her tongue, more like ice than spun sugar.

Next to the enormous oak slab of a front door sat a white stone pitcher, a sturdy, tiger-orange mum spilling over the sides. Per the instructions she'd copied down from the house-sitting ad, she tilted it carefully, grunting with its weight. A silver key rested in the center of a dark square of mildew on the concrete.

Val snatched it and slid the key into the front door's lock. She needed to lean her shoulder against the door to push it open; when she did, it was as if the dark wood was pushing her back. Inside, the air conditioner blasted. The frosty climate of the white marble foyer stung her nostrils.

Val stepped cautiously into the foyer, taking care to wipe her shoes on the mat four times more than she would have anywhere else. The entryway hosted immaculate, gleaming floors, rich mahogany tables, a crystal chandelier, a plush, moss-green carpet with fresh vacuum tracks that coated the stairs leading up to the second-floor landing.

Luxurious—terrifyingly luxurious, where the hell *was* she —, but the dark mouth of the landing felt strange. Heavy.

For a second, she tasted basement musk at the back of her throat.

She didn't belong here, that was clear, but the second floor seemed to repel her, push her away with the density of its darkness, the stairs' degree of incline a spatial formula to keep her out.

The ad hadn't said anything about her actual housesitting duties, but she hadn't read much farther than $1k CASH, ONE NIGHT ONLY. As she walked through the first-floor rooms: a dining room, an enormous farm kitchen, a small sunroom, and a sitting room complete with stereotypical tobacco-and-leather man-cave-fineries, it was clear that the owner of Lion's Head had neither animals nor plants. It was obviously well-maintained, likely by a staff, but it was silent now, dormant.

Val assumed she was supposed to watch the house so that kids wouldn't mess with it tonight—wouldn't egg it or throw toilet paper rolls up into the cream-colored gutters. Val could guess how they felt, trying to reabsorb the beacon of wealth that overlooked their community like a prison warden into the realm of lower-middle-class normalcy.

Did its occupants not eat eggs? Use toilet paper?

Val checked her phone. No bars. She didn't know the WiFi password, but Val hadn't seen a computer, or a television, or even a landline, let alone a router. Through the floor-to-ceiling windows of the sitting room, she watched the half-naked canopy swallow the sun.

The sketchy, anonymous online posting, the cash offer, the isolation... had she learned nothing from those years with Iggy? Cash exchanging hands, still flecked with blood fresh enough to smear; couches crusted with the same foam that clung to blue lips; the glassy, vacant eyes that followed her movements even now.

If she died here, who would even know?

She swallowed the thought so hard her throat spasmed.

And then she saw the stack of hundreds on the Noguchi coffee table.

She glanced from the wad of money to her inert phone, then to the plush leather couches, the real wood-burning fireplace, and, polished wood glistening like topaz, a personal bar.

Goosebumps erupted on the back of her neck and the basement girls' eyes, all twenty-six of them, peered out at her from over the bar's marble top, waiting to see what she'd do like they always did.

The first time she'd had a drink, she was 12. That was when she met Iggy—basement party of a friend of a friend, turning her head away from the dipping torsos and tiny hills of white powder on most if not all of the surfaces, all dark lighting and neon body paint, bass hammering in her ears, loud enough to rattle her teeth. He'd acted removed from the scene, even embarrassed, that first time, but he wasn't, not really. Even though she sank more and more into the drink and the drugs as Iggy fell in love with her malleability and acidic mouth, and the basement transitioned from party space to hellish storage, Val knew she could navigate it blindfolded, to this day.

She needed the money, indisputably. Without it, no transmission repair. No Darcey, maybe forever. She'd done worse for cash.

Val ground her teeth and set to work building a fire with the neat stack of pre-chopped, grocery store logs on the hearth. Once built, she sat on the leather couch, focusing on the flames. If only the huge windows had shades—they were gaping, empty eyeholes into the syrupy black of the night on the hill, staring into the woods blindly.

Once Val had allowed herself to forgo time completely, her phone placed screen-side-down on the glass of the coffee table, she sauntered, casual and aloof, to the bar.

She hadn't had a drink since the night it happened—since the basement girls became the dead girls and Iggy tasted the metal of his own Glock—but some top-shelf vodka was chilling in the freezer compartment of the mini-fridge.

Every half hour or so, she re-opened the mini-fridge to remind herself that *just in case* the night closes in too heavy, *just in case* the basement girls get too close, *just in case* the road back to Darcey ends up being too long...

The grandfather clock in the corner of the room struck midnight and she heard a single, high-pitched beep, metallic slide, and *click* resonate from the foyer.

Val went through each of the rooms on the lower floor, scanning for cameras in the corners, hidden devices, or out-of-date smoke detectors that could have made the noise. She clicked each light on, then quickly off as the rooms were cleared. Not because she gave a shit about a probably-billionaire's electric bill, but because she felt like she was in an aquarium tank, invisible night-patrons pressing their noses to the glass of the windows.

Scurrying back to the fire through the dark rooms, she threw another log on and decided to leave the soft orange backlighting of the bar on as well.

None of the girls in prison knew she was afraid of the dark, but the dark reminded her of vanishing into burlap, trying to blink away too many shots, silence except for the shuffling of bodies at the bottom of the stairs that smelled like they were already dead. She'd watched a girl from her pod go up in flames when she fell asleep with a contraband lighter in her hand.

Val pulled a scratchy throw blanket over herself and breathed through the urge to get up and check the bottle again when a knock came from the entryway.

It wasn't kids because they'd vandalize under a cloak of darkness; it wasn't the police because there were no lights; it wasn't her parole officer because she didn't know where Val was; it wasn't her mother because she'd given up on her a long time ago.

Val squirmed further into the couch, flush with the cushions, unmoving.

The knock came again, this time harder, irregular in beat, like someone weakly throwing their shoulder against a wall.

She slid down from the couch and crawled over to the fireplace, sliding the poker off its hook. Keeping low to the floor, she crawled across varnished wood, then freezing white marble. She stood against the door, grainy oak flush with her strong back, and looked out the peephole.

The front step was empty—her Accent, in plain view, unbothered through the thin veil of night.

Val grabbed the door handle, slid the deadlock over, and yanked, the barrage of threats and false bravado for the intruder bubbling up the back of her throat, but choked on it when the door didn't budge.

She pulled on the door again, jostling it slightly in its frame, but it did not open. She clicked the deadbolt over, back, over, back, tug—it was locked from deeper inside the door than she could reach. *Beep, sliiide, click.*

Every window Val tried—the kitchen, the sunroom, the sitting room—was painted shut with gorgeous high-gloss white, cold panes rooted in thick wooden frames.

The pile of hundreds in the center of the coffee table chuckled.

The knock came again, and Val crept back to the entryway.

Thud, thud, pause, thud.

Directly above her head, too muffled to be coming from the second floor, loud enough to be coming from inside the house. The attic.

Another knock, just one, followed by a groan—thin and watery and childlike, the sound a toddler makes before they throw up, telling their mothers, *help, help me.*

Val remembered handing Darcey to her mother that last time. She was doped up and hammered out of her mind, Iggy's stolen car parked halfway on the lawn, but she'd done it. She'd gotten Darcey out before she'd been able to reach the doorknobs, because one of them in that house led down. Val knew if Darcey saw the basement girls she'd become one herself. That's why Val had always kept the lights off when she'd descended.

She'd handed Darcey to her mother, a faceless, backlit silhouette with a voice like caramel the second after its started to burn. She'd kissed her baby's forehead, smelled lollipop on her breath.

Valeria, you know this is it, right?

Val had been hoping so for a while now.

Her mother had called the cops that night. Her father had been perched in the window, writing down Iggy's long-elusive license plate number. She'd still been a kid then, only 15, so the kidnapping charges would have stuck if Iggy hadn't...

Val's stomach flipped at the memory. The noise came again—a weak beating of fists on wood, a tiny, squeaking cry.

Val knew that people with money like this could do things just as fucked up as poor people like Iggy could. A lot of the time—worse. A kid tied up in the attic? Some pervert's fantasy, or an unfortunate, genetic-lottery-losing heir apparent? It wouldn't surprise her.

Were doped-up teenagers different than little kids and hooking? Was drug money different than familial shame and ill-wrought inheritance? Val ventured that if you poured them all out on the pavement they'd splash the same shade of red.

The knocking moved over the dining room now, followed by a long, whispering scrape. Someone dragging themselves along the floor, another strangled yelp following the movement. The first cry Darcey let loose into the world.

Val threw herself up the stairs, a cold sweat exploding from her pores. She took them two at a time, and when she reached the landing, she saw doors down either side of the hall, each thrown open in cold invitation.

Val felt along the wall next to the stairs and found the light switch. When she flicked it, nothing happened.

She swallowed the *of fucking course.*

Through the dim light of the driveway that trickled through the window at the end of the hall, she saw a square cutout of an attic door, the access rope dangling low, almost to the floor.

Val approached it slowly, her feet cushioned by the thick-pile carpet, her eyes rapidly attempting to adjust to the darkness that seemed to pulsate from the open doors around her. She grabbed the pull-cord. It was braided, soft, velvety. She tugged on it and the well-oiled ladder unfolded itself gracefully from the ceiling like a développé.

The sounds from the attic stopped abruptly.

"Hello?" she called up, taking her first step.

Rungs up an attic ladder, rotted stairs up from a basement. Attic boys and basement girls and everyone else is lost in the shuffle. Val grabbed the ladder's frame, vision spinning. She wouldn't turn away this time. She'd save this kid like she saved Darcey. She felt the basement girls watching her from down the hall, back where she'd come.

As she neared the scuttle hole, brief orange flickers made their way down to her eyes and brightened as her vision adjusted.

The attic was illuminated by what must have been fifty candles, some enormous that had likely been burning for days, some smaller, almost entirely burnt out. Some wicks were still standing in a shallow pool of melted wax. They'd been lit just before her arrival.

Val took in the small room with the unusual cathedral ceiling; walls of stone that lifted into black nothingness. She'd never seen an attic like this before in her life. It reminded her of cloying incense, flavorless wafers. The stagnant air smelled like the time her cousin Martine had gotten a nail through her foot and didn't treat the festering hole for weeks.

An enormous, gilded chair loomed in the corner, molten and liquid in the candlelight. Small tables surrounding the chair were draped in beautiful swathes of fabric and ancient silks. A mountain of coins was heaped at the base of the seat, golds and silvers and bronzes shimmering with borrowed flame. Tapestries and shields with a family crest, the head of a roaring lion framed in black and burgundy.

Sculptures of obsidian caught what little light there was and swallowed it: a woman carrying a bowl on her head, something lumpy and shapeless inside; an enormous, upright alligator with the head of a peacock; a man with a sword, pommel between outward, steepled hands, tip pressed downward against the pedestal, hand over his heart, headless.

"Hello?" Val called again. Every step she took into the attic shot electricity through her feet. Without the drugs and the booze she felt the slow, nauseating unfurling of *something is wrong.*

Val looked at the tile floor as she approached the chair. Every other tile or so was hand-painted, depicting a scene. Most of them featured a shapeless, fleshy lump with a thin neck snaking from somewhere in the center, a man's head with a sideways face grinning up at her. In the images, it held sheaves of wheat, ankles of babies, piles of gold spilling from too many hands, a dripping human heart.

A sound again, small, from the corner of the room, behind the throne.

A baby's gurgle, a woman's throaty laugh, a man's scream, a person singing to themselves, quietly, rocking, long after their baby has fallen asleep. A coyote's chilling song from those nights in the woods she'd spent after being released, shivering, back pressed up against a 24-hour diner, rocking, too scared to go in. Too scared to be seen for the monster she was.

A hand snaked itself out from behind the throne, connected to an impossibly thin wrist, and grabbed the golden back of it. Two eyes with smoldering red irises, black where they should have been white, peered out from the space between the chair's back and seat.

Val's scream caught in her throat, her body frozen.

Arm over arm, leg over leg, its body an enormous, bubbling mass of flesh; it pulled itself up over the seat of the chair and inspected Val, jagged sideways mouth emitting the coos of an infant and the screech of an eagle amid prehistoric clicks from its long, thin neck.

They locked eyes and she felt raw power rolling from it in waves. She tasted toasted golden fields of prosperity, fragrant, piquant waves of rival blood. The arresting officer, the judge, her mother, her father, Iggy, the basement girls.

She shook her head violently and retched. No, not them.

It grew tired of observing.

For how bulbous it was, it moved as quickly as falling water. Her instinct was to roll.

The creature sliced through the air behind her and spun fluidly, centering its gaze on her as she crawled toward the attic ladder.

It screeched, a cacophony of babies and women and men and persons and the sands of time and tectonic plates rubbing against one another. Val finally did scream, blood erupting from her ears.

It scrabbled toward her, smiling vacantly with its rows of grey tombstone teeth. Val hurled herself toward the statues. She grabbed the pommel of the headless man's sword—the blind leading the blind—and yanked it out from between his yielding hands with a scrape.

Gracias a Dios.

It was decorative, but real metal and sharp. She rounded, holding it out in front of her, knowing full well she'd never held any weapon except for Iggy's Glock when he got scared he'd shoot all the basement girls before he could sell them.

He'd been a shivering mess, pacing from grimy mattress to window, smoking another hit of meth as he peered through the plastic blinds, waiting for the red and blue flashes.

Shoot me, Valeria, just shoot me!

Fifteen-year-old Val, pregnant, eyes running with tears and nose running with snot, sitting on the gun so he couldn't pry it from her as easy, praying the safety was on.

The creature moved forward until the tip of the sword pressed into its flesh, a single spot of black ooze pooling around the tip. It smelled like rosewater and gasoline. It leaned its face close to Val's, head wobbling on its thin neck. Its breath stank of carrion. Again, she felt a wave of longing wash through her. She felt the urge to touch its slick hide. It smiled lazily, reeling her in.

It made another sound, like Darcey, hungry in the black morning hours. The trance broken, Val shoved the blade forward with all her might and sliced downward, cutting another shriek from the creature as ichor spilled to the floor. Val's ears pulsed dangerously and she smelled copper. A hot droplet slid down the contour of her jaw and neck.

Staggering into the tables, Val snatched up a silk and wrapped it around her arm, then turned to face the monster.

It was in the position she had left it, curled into itself, the substance dripping from its middle, pooling around its feet smelling less like roses and more like gasoline by the second.

It twisted its head from one side to the other like a snake tasting the air, mouth still a grin, eyes lidless.

Two centuries have passed since I have been offered someone worthy. You smell like the others, but you are different—aren't you, Valeria?

The voice was a whisper, cool and seductive, beautiful even, and it bounced around the inside of Val's head as if the thought was her own. It took two steps to the left and Val moved to the right—a wide, slow circle.

When this family earned me as its patron, they were warriors. Strong. I made them stronger, and they nourished me. But their offspring are weak. Pitiful. It spat a large glob of reeking murk onto the tiles. Softened and made useless by my opulence. They no longer perform the rites. They no longer take heads in my name.

Val continued placing one foot behind, one foot ahead, a sideways crouch toward the wall of candles.

But you, Valeria. I know the heads that you have taken.

The basement girls watched, blankly, through the attic's hatch.

I can make you even stronger. I can fulfill your desires.

The taste of warm, mulled wine exploded on her tongue, slid down her throat. Her mouth watered helplessly. It chuckled, the sound of stones thrown into a woodchipper.

Do you see? Leave mortality; walk with my blood in your veins. Leave your fears and weaknesses on this plane, with the unworthy.

A thick, black tongue unfurled from its mouth and licked ooze from its teeth. It took a step forward into the center of the circle. Val's pulse quickened and she quickly sidestepped twice more. The heat from the candles pressed against her back.

Leave everything. Empty yourself for nothing but me, and I can make you as a god.

Its voice held the sharp promise of a vodka shot, the warmth of knife-scarred hands, the lilt of false adoration, but there was nothing left to leave behind. She'd known what it was like to be emptied for someone, and the unquenchable thirst to be full of herself again.

Everything that mattered was in front of her—just a little further down the road.

Val flicked the length of silk from her forearm and touched it to one of the candle flames, watching the fine threads sizzle and pop as they caught. Fingertips burning, she threw the fiery offering at the creature.

It stuck to its front, searing the flesh with a hiss.

It screamed as it fell to its spindly knees, batting furiously at the still-burning fabric adhered to its skin.

Val shot forward, blade-first, and ran through its gelatinous body over and over until her hands were sticking to the grip and her feet were sticking to the tile, ichor obscuring everything. Hot putrescence shot from its dying form like a geyser, slicking her hair, leaving her with nothing but the whites of her eyes in the darkness.

The creature laid in a heap, unmoving, but Val sawed the ornamental sword's edge against its cord-like neck and severed the head entirely, just in case. It felt like the right way to kill a god and ensure it doesn't come back looking for you.

The ichor began to catch fire like pitch. Val panted; the heat was overwhelming. If it touched her, she'd be a torch. She backed herself towards the attic's hatch. The basement girls were gone.

She climbed down as tongues of flame began to lick the opening, ran through the lush carpeting and down the stairs, outrunning her funeral pyre.

The thousand dollars was still sitting on the coffee table. Val snatched it, pocketed it. Her throat was hot; the smoke was starting to fill the lower rooms. She looked over at the bar, thought of the vodka in the freezer.

Let it burn.

Val darted across the foyer into the dining room and picked up a leather upholstered chair with burnished iron legs. She hefted it onto her right shoulder, then threw it as hard as she could at the window.

The glass didn't break, but a hairline crack split the pane into six jagged sections. She coughed as smoke spilled down the stairs. Every smoke detector was screaming.

Val lifted the chair again, head swimming. She threw it at the window, heard the sound of glass shattering, and crawled out into the night, hissing as she felt the skin of her palms and forearms tear.

She ran to her Accent, unlocked the doors, and cursed at it until the engine turned over, then drove down the winding driveway until she reached the gates, which opened automatically at her presence. Lion's Head was an explosion of sunset colors, the moon watching over its demise. Val watched it burn through her rearview mirror, heart pounding, until she was sure it couldn't be saved—until she was sure she couldn't go back and change her mind.

The gas tank was nearly empty, the transmission had about ten miles left on it—at most—but the cash in her pocket felt as heavy and comforting as a full stomach. A fixed car, gas, a meal, maybe a rest-stop present for Darcey. Maybe something for her mom and dad. What could you get from a rest stop that adequately portrayed *I'm sorry I fucked everything up?*

A group of teenagers, out past their curfew and wearing masks a day early, stood across the street, watching the blaze. A bottle of vodka lay discarded by their feet. No one was out looking for them.

Val felt a tug, umbilical, calling her from the east. She turned her wheel away from burning attics and basements, bottles and bodies exploding from heat and pressure.

Val turned toward the life she'd saved, and the life she was saving.

H. Marin (she/they) is a disabled queer author of dark speculative fiction. She is the former Managing Editor of Radon Journal, and in her freelance editing work champions marginalized narratives. She is a current MFA candidate at Fairfield University living in New England with her partner in literature and in life, her two children, and her two black cats. Read her work in Night Shades Magazine and forthcoming in If There's Anyone Left and Pulp Asylum, among others. Follow her on Bluesky at hanmarin@bsky.social, and find more from her at https://hmarinliterary.com/.

Silent Disco
by A.J. Hodges

"Oi, Paul. You coming to the demo?"

I press the phone against my face. It's Sabeena. My best friend a.k.a. boundary pusher. I slink over to my bedroom window and hush my voice. "What demo," I whisper. "I've got college all day today."

She's always getting me into trouble.

"Sack college. This is more important. Roko Industries got planning approval."

"So?"

"They're building more skyscrapers. We can kiss goodbye to social housing anywhere near the center."

Her words and enthusiasm drift over me, but they don't land. I'm honestly not sure what she means. I just know it's *politics*, Sabeena's number one topic.

Except for clubbing, that is.

"I can't," I say firmly. "We're still on for tonight though, right?"

"Of course." Sabeena's grin is as big as mine, I just know it.

"See you there then." I pause. "Oh, and let me know how the demo goes."

She's always trying to rope me into some new venture. Sometimes I say yes. But not right now. The thing is, ever since I've been hanging out with Sabeena, I've been falling behind with college. Last week Ms. McDonnell called me into her office. If my grades slip an inch further or I miss another day, I'm out.

It all started when I bumped into her in Piccadilly Gardens last summer, for like the first time ever. I'd just bought a new pair of baggy trousers from Afflecks, this dock-off alternative market in the Northern Quarter, when —yes—I tripped over them. Sabeena helped me up, her green eyes sparkling above her dark freckles and olive skin when she saw my Cradle of Filth T-shirt. We went for coffee, and we've been inseparable ever since.

Sabeena introduced me to Rockworld, this club that stays open all night on Fridays. It quickly became our second home. First there was the honeymoon phase. And now? Who am I kidding, I still love it. But twelve hours until doors open. Ugh. I have to make it through advanced math and double German first.

Friday *always* drags.

After six hours of deathly boring calculus and subjunctives, I finally make it to the train station. A cold wind rips up, shaking the sad flowerpots. Not the weather to be marching on a demo.

On the opposite platform, three young teens dressed in The North Face jackets, baseball caps, and tracksuit bottoms heckle me. "You fucking goth. Are you a fag?"

I bite my lip, trying not to laugh at their stupid performance. I raise my middle finger as the train pulls into the station. They're yelling, causing a scene now, but I don't care. The train will depart in seconds.

I sit down and inhale the train chair smell—cleaning fluid mixed with stale school dinners. Then I rub the manky condensation off the window and scowl at them. Mascara, glow bands, and bright-blue hair is too much for them, I get that. The train shunts off and matchbox houses pass me by, depressing at any time of year, but especially bleak in the January darkness.

Me and Sabeena love Rockworld because it isn't like other clubs in Manchester. The music is wicked. *What I like about it there*, I remember Sabeena saying, *is that it's so relaxed. You can be anything you want to be.*

But Rockworld isn't without its issues. Some people just go there to take drugs. We call them the Spaceheads, and I give them a wide berth. Then there's the straight-edge crew —mostly former Spaceheads. They pride themselves on making it through to the end of the night drug-free. Like what an achievement.

My favorite group is the die-hard fans, the Metalheads. They're mint because they love the music. And fun to hang out with except when dropping irritating factoids about their favorite bands.

Occasionally a scally or posh kid from the suburbs drops in. They usually assimilate fast or leave twice as quickly as they arrive.

And our crew? We're kinda in the middle. Social butterflies, that's us. There's one person I really dislike, though. This Spacehead called Lucy. Okay, so maybe I'm jealous because Sabeena's started hanging out with her more, but something's not right about her. And I don't want Sabeena getting into drugs.

The train blasts into Manchester Oxford Road Station and Sabeena's waiting for me on the platform, snowflakes melting on her faux-fur-lined hoodie and jeans. It's never *that* cold here, but when it snows, everything feels peaceful and your bones ache like mad.

"All right," I say with a grin. Sabeena *is* my Manchester this last six months. People think we must be dating. If I weren't like 90 percent into guys, I would be down with that, but we're besties.

"How's it going," I say, flashing her a cheeky grin.

She scowls, like she's had a shite day at college. "Same old. It feels like ages since I saw you last."

I chuckle. "It wasn't *that* long ago. Sounds like you need to chill."

I'd seen her last Saturday, when we got chucked out of the Arndale for some low-level thieving (only from corporations, mind) and loitering, sliding down the escalator rails to Market Street.

Sabeena always pushes things a bit too far. Especially on nights out. And me? I let her. I'm the one who has to pull back, stop things from getting too out of control. And I can't let that happen, with all the trouble I'm in at college. But Fridays are my release.

Sabeena straightens her back. "Listen up, mister, you need to relax too. You'll nail the exams."

I nod slowly, and we mooch on down the stairs packed tight against the viaduct, which shudders as a train arrives. The dark, the lights, the snow, and her coat create an electricity. But as we scoot into the shadows, I can't help but feel that something is slightly off. Something I can't put my finger on.

"Wait up," a voice shouts from behind me. I spin around to face the Salisbury—this pub where the Spaceheads hang out before clubbing—and spot Lucy.

My eyes narrow. "I thought we were gonna meet you there?" She's at least five years older than us, which is also a bit sus if you ask me.

Lucy beams a fake smile at me, then a warmer one at Sabeena. "I texted, said I'd come to the station."

"Right," I say casually, judging her with my stare. She's trouble.

I look up to Oxford Road, where young women in short skirts and heavy makeup are keeping pace with men in designer shirts. So binary. My mind shoots back to the stupid scallies at the station.

The snow gets a little heavier.

"The Salisbury looks dead," I say, nodding at the pub. "Maybe the Spaceheads have *actually* gone inside and bought something?"

Lucy huffs. I really wish I could figure her out. But I can't deny it, she has this charm, this energy. Green eyes, purple hair dye, skin paler even than mine, and with bloodred lipstick. Lucy is hot, there's no denying that. I don't say it though—calling yourself bi or pan is trendy here, and I'm anti-the-alternative-mainstream, if that's even a thing.

Sabeena folds her arms together, teeth chattering. "It's too fucking cold to chill outside here anyway. Can we go straight to Rockworld?"

Lucy nods firmly. "Wise move," she says, glaring at me.

Unwise move, I think. Talking at me like I'm under her thumb.

Sabeena starts walking. "Wait. I need something light to eat, and sugar for later, to keep me awake." She grabs my arm and pulls it toward her warm, furry coat, the tips of the fur damp with melted snow. "Come on, this week's gonna be special."

"Just don't go disappearing on me this time." *Especially not with her.* I roll my eyes. Last week she vanished for ages, then told me this mad story about a hidden room in the club. I spent the whole time looking for her, but nothing. "Why did you do that?"

She hesitates, then her green eyes lock with mine. "I'm sorry, I—you know how time just flies there? I—" She brushes a thick snowflake off her faux-fur hoodie. "This week we'll hang out together all night."

I smile, all smug, at Lucy.

We head past the Palace Theatre, smartly dressed people queuing to get in, some shivering in the cold, others wrapped up in thick coats, then arrive at the familiar Tesco store and make our way inside.

The bright light makes me wince. I'm a wannabe vampire, after all.

Okay, so the blue hair is achingly pop punk, but I'll dye it black again next year for Halloween.

A tropical blast blows bakery smells around the entrance, and my stomach rumbles. Sabeena and Lucy speed around the aisles, picking up jelly beans, water, and some chewing gum and vapor rub for the Spaceheads. I don't know why Sabeena looks up to them, and to Lucy. They're kind of sad. But she's a dabbler, an experimenter. I am, too, but I have to be more cautious right now.

We leave, head back out into the arctic chill, then dive down an alleyway next to the supermarket, proper hidden. Lucy taps on a black door and a tiny Plexiglass window opens. The moment they see us, the door swings open.

Rockworld is Manchester's open secret.

We inch through the door.

It slams shut behind us.

Dum, dum, dum.

I snap my eyes shut for a second and let the bass filter through my mind. Then I hold out my hand and place it on Sabeena's shoulder. We continue down a dark corridor, through a foyer with navy-blue ceilings and tired red paint peeling off the walls, then hotfoot it to the main room.

I take in the surroundings. The room is packed with goths, punks, emos, mosh kids. Spaceheads and Metalheads all mixed together. Everyone dancing at their own rhythm, heavy metal beats leaching out through massive speakers.

"Are you okay, mate?" A finger pokes me in the stomach. "Know where I can get any pills?"

Fuckin Spaceheads. "Not my poison," I reply, forcing a smile. I take a step back and the green-haired grunger wanders off. The music alone carries you through till dawn.

My mind flashes back to last week. *Just try half of one*, Sabeena had said, crumbling a pink speckled pill she called a unicorn with her thumb. I flashed her an evil glare. She took it anyway, and *that's* when she disappeared.

I felt used, dropped by her.

"We stay together tonight," I repeat, biting my lip. "And no pills. They don't suit you."

She nods slowly. "We agreed," she replies. "And I respect that."

I grab her hand. We dance by the massive speakers, then slink over to a row of tired black leather barstools beside a billiard table. A slender punk with a green mohawk is playing against a butch goth in a corset and short tartan skirt. It's not clear who is winning. The music switches to nu-metal, and I groan. The grunge teens—surfing on the giant bass speakers, hands outstretched—quickly exit the room.

I order a cranberry juice and vodka, slump into a sofa, and relax. Eventually, "Closer" by Nine Inch Nails plays. I get up and dance with Sabeena and Lucy, our bodies rocking to the beat.

We exit the main room via the dance floor and head to the foyer, inhaling its peeling black linoleum and red-painted walls. It's full of teenagers and mosh kids, chilling out and chatting among themselves. In one corner there's a bunch of emo kids with carefully styled black hair and rainbow bracelets. By the ancient Pac-Man machine, a couple of goths in their early thirties are hanging out.

Sabeena catches my gaze. "Wanna go dance? It's gabber hour in the goth room?"

That stuff is hardcore. Hard pass from me. "I'll sit this one out."

"OK," Lucy says, with too much enthusiasm. "See you later."

Lucy winks at Sabeena, then the pair disappear into the screaming gloom of the goth room. A sick feeling creeps across my stomach, remembering last week. I'm paranoid she'll disappear again. And this place, alive with new faces every week, but longtime clubbers aren't coming as much as they used to. As if they're disappearing.

I should just chill here in the foyer. But I get up anyway.

I shuffle out along the corridor, then take a sharp left turn into a room coated in ultraviolet paint. Lasers cut through the dark, a violet UV glow emerging from the ceiling. An angel in white spandex is drinking Newcastle Brown ale from a bottle. I look down, my black hoodie now coated with speckles dancing in the UV light. I pull my hoodie up over my face and sit down at a table, trying to be as inconspicuous as possible... but let's be honest, the room is small.

A few songs later, Lucy and Sabeena rock up to my table and take a seat.

Lucy gets straight to it. "Lighten up, Paul." She flashes me an ice-cold glare, then fishes a small plastic bag out of her pocket. She forms a cup with her hand, then half a pill, white with blue speckles, a teddy bear imprinted on it, drops into her palm.

"I know what you're looking for. A trip someplace. Take this, and I'll show you." My fist clenches. I know Lucy is aware I could get chucked out of college, and she's suggesting this? I'd never accept dodgy drugs from anyone, let alone her. But Sabeena looks at me pleadingly. Part of me wants to play along, for her sake.

Sabeena seriously needs to audit her friends here.

Lucy drops the crumbling pill onto my palm. I stick my tongue out and place it on there, then I close my mouth and deftly stick it under my tongue. As soon as Sabeena and Lucy leave to dance again, I subtly spit it out.

We dance. I feel nothing.

Then things happen fast. Lucy nudges me, beckons us both to follow her. I swear she studies my eyes carefully—I have no idea what she's looking for. We move back out to the foyer.

"You, stay here," she says.

Sabeena's buzzing, dancing, full of energy.

"I think we should go home," I say to Sabeena, my eyes locked on Lucy. "Together."

"Sabeena go home? In that state? No chance," Lucy replies. She taps my shoulder. "You need to take a seat. And chill."

The bass thuds.

Dum, dum, dum.

I get up to protest, but Lucy knocks me down.

"We'll be back soon."

They leave and I follow them again, letting the crowd swallow me up. I feel like the decisions I make right now— heck—the decision to even be here, is shaping my future in ways I can't imagine. I make a beeline for the main room, where I'd sworn a secret door had been the week before. But nothing. This club is confusing, a labyrinth. But a building layout can't change from week to week. Can it?

I rap my fist against the wall, but it feels solid. An emo kid flashes me a glance, assuming I must be a Spacehead.

I wander through the corridors again, super busy now, looking for them both. Last week, Sabeena just reappeared. That's all I can hope for now.

I glance down at my watch.

02:37.

Still pretty early, yet the club feels emptier than usual. I find a quiet corner so I can make a plan to find Sabeena. I've asked *everyone* I know here.

I squint, then by the massive speakers, maybe twenty meters away from me, I spot Lucy. Alone.

I dart over. "What's going on?" I say. "Where's Sabeena?"

Stone-faced, she says, "Come with me." She holds out a pair of earmuffs. "Put these on. I'll take you to Sabeena."

She lifts a hand, beckons for me to follow her. And then everything goes black.

I come round, vision blurry. I'm in a dark, confined space, like a shed or—oh my god, this is a DJ booth. The earmuffs lie on the floor beside me. A black tatty leather barstool looms to my left, above it DJ decks. In the upper far corner above the decks, TV screens flash images of the different rooms. I stare, half hypnotized. The main room is near-empty—it must be late. I pad my pockets, searching for my mobile.

It's not there.

What the fuck?

I try to stand up, but my legs are weak. This has to be Lucy, her stupid teddy bear pill. I grab the edge of the work surface, haul myself up, then spin around, away from the monitors, the chair. Plexiglass cuts my booth off from the dance floor. When I see the scene before me, I freeze.

A group of people, at least twenty, are on the dance floor. But they're not dancing, not moving. I don't think they can see me. Their eyes are glazed over, unblinking. But that's not the maddest thing about them.

They are completely frozen, arms locked into contorted positions. I focus and make out the hairs on one guy's arm, like an insect trapped in amber. Pale faces, some mouths clamped into a laugh or grin, others scared. More than spooked—they look petrified.

A sick feeling shoots up from the pit of my stomach. And then, near the back of the room, jammed among them, I see a pair of green eyes staring back at me—Sabeena.

Catatonic.

That's the word my psychology teacher used once. Locked in position, like someone took a photo of them dancing. Disco lights flash red and purple and blue.

"Sabeena," I cry out, rapping my hands against the Plexiglass.

I swear her left eye twitched when I shouted, but I honestly have no idea if she can hear me. I shout out, wave, but no reaction. I cast my gaze around the room. It's as if each person's soul has been ripped away.

This place is messed up.

I scan around, searching for a way out, then throw my weight against the booth door. Lucy must have brought me here. But why here? Why not the dance floor? My mind flits back to what happened in the goth room. *I spat out the pill.* I look around the booth for some clue, anything that will help me. The DJ decks—controls? *Maybe Lucy didn't bank on me waking up.*

Whatever, I can't take any risks now.

My bottom lip is moist, metallic, and salty. I dab it. Blood drips off my finger. I glance up again at the monitors and search through the live feed, through all the different rooms. Then I see her.

Lucy's in the main room, talking with what looks like one of the club bouncers.

Frantic, I punch several buttons on the DJ decks. The colored lights move and muffled music blasts out through the speakers. Red shifts to green, strobe lights flicker, and the frozen dancers shift to a fresh position, catatonic again. The flashing makes their bodies shake and arms jerk, in a cruelly fragile way. Panicking, I turn the strobe lights off, and they freeze again.

The eerie thing is, despite the smiles, the grins, the fear and despair on their faces, they strike me as emotionless.

I try knocking on the glass again.

"Sabeena, Sabeena!"

But nothing.

Desperate, I punch all the buttons. Then, at the back of the room, I see the wall start to move. I crouch.

It's Lucy. She's wearing earmuffs too, but hers are pink, not black like everyone else's.

She cannot see me. Or can she?

She stops in front of a grunge rocker dressed in an old Nirvana T-shirt. *Heart-Shaped Box.*

Now she's heading over here. I'm on the floor already, hiding, biting my lip again. I peek up, my gaze just reaching the bottom of the Plexiglass. She can't see me. No. Or she's pretending not to. It's like she's checking things, treating the clubbers like robots, like objects that need fixing. She's *studying* them.

I lean back and consider my options. My best strategy is to play unconscious. I hear the jangle of keys, the door creaks open. I sit stock-still, my eyes near-closed.

Lucy sold drugs to the Spaceheads, that much I knew. She kinda fit in here, but also didn't. I know that feeling.

But this room, this place—it's another level of dark.

I stay mock unconscious as she places the earmuffs over my ears again. I hear a crackle, then a deep voice whispers to me, tells me to stand. I get up, afraid of what might happen if I don't.

My little finger starts to shake. Lucy can't see that. I must walk mechanically. I lurch forward, out of the booth, and the voice leads me to a spot on the dance floor. Lucy is back in the booth, but I can't see her now. All I see is a mirror and the light and colors. The lights begin to flash and then red, green, purple dots appear in front of my eyes. I can feel myself being lulled into a gentle trance, but I fight it.

If I go under, how can I help Sabeena, help everyone else? The strobe lighting flickers, drawing me into a trance, but I keep struggling against it.

My finger starts to twitch again. Shit. She can't notice. I think of school, of college, the deep mess I'm in right now, and I laugh. If I get out of here, I ain't never coming back.

Then Lucy dashes off, disappearing through a door at the back of the room.

This is my last chance, my only chance. I need to bring Sabeena out of this trance, and we need to get out of here to safety. I rip off the headphones, run over to her, and wave in her face.

Nothing.

"Wake up, wake up," I say.

Nothing.

Stomach heavy, I leg it back to the booth. This time, Lucy's left the door open. Schoolgirl error. I dart to the controls and search for the strobe button. I press it, and everyone shifts position. She's left a silver business card on the side. *Roko Industries.* The pieces start to connect.

I rush back to Sabeena, wave, shout, remove her headphones, play punch her. Still nothing.

"Last resort," I mutter, then sock her a punch to the stomach. She gasps, then stares at me. "Where am I?"

It worked! "Not sure," I say. "But we have to get out of here. Fast."

"Lucy said we're going to the fourth room, a fourth room?"

"This is the fourth room, for sure. And we need to leave. *Now.*"

Sabeena looks around. "Why are these people standing like statues? What's going on?"

I bite my lip. "I'm not sure. Some kind of experiment? Lucy... she works for the developers. The same ones you were protesting against. Come on." I zip toward the door.

"We can't leave these people here, not like this."

A pang of guilt surges through me. "It's not safe here."

Sabeena walks over to the guy in the Heart-Shaped Box T-shirt. "We have to try."

A creak at the back of the room. A door opening.

"We need to leave," I mouth.

Lucy blocks the exit.

"Stop," she says. "You've seen too much."

"Too much?" I scramble for words. "What the hell is this place?"

"Some questions are better left unanswered," Lucy says, seething.

"Try me." I hold my palms out. "It's not like we're going anywhere. You've won. So try me."

Lucy scowls. "Your counterculture is destroying the city. Waifs and strays on the streets, graffiti, drugged out people polluting the city center."

"You're the one handing out pills."

"Pills aren't the problem." Lucy says, proper dismissive, then pulls out a knife. "So I'll ask you just once to put the headphones back on."

I stare at the headphones. Fuck. "Sabeena," I grit out. "The headphones!" I turn to Lucy. "You can't kidnap people, bring them here like this."

Lucy points at the frozen people. "These young people, they all have creativity we can use to rebuild the city, make it a better place. That's what the headphones are harnessing. And we're keeping them safe, off the streets—"

"Now!" I shout at Sabeena and rush forward, knocking Lucy over, pushing through the door and out, out into a hidden corner of the goth room. "The doors, quick!" I scream.

A sick feeling creeps over me again. The club owners must be in on this. And they have bouncers, security.

The club's nearly empty, the music downbeat, just the dregs remaining. A few people dancing to an old Cranberries track; a handful of strung-out goths and moshers scattered around on tables and chairs or slumped against walls.

We lurch toward the foyer, and I grab Sabeena's hand. I run out of the club, dragging Sabeena with me. Lucy stops at the club entrance. "You can't leave this club. Not really," she shouts.

*

It's still dark when we rush out of Rockworld, not looking back, the now-thick dusting of snow slowing our progress. We push through a bunch of rave kids. A Spacehead goth chewing on a pacifier, a green-haired punk cradling a teddy bear. We skid forward, pushing toward St Peter's Square.

Sabeena takes the lead. We take a sharp turn into an alley then another, then down by the canal, making sure we've lost Lucy. We end up in Chinatown, the bakery just setting up for the day, blowing a sweet doughy scent. I try to catch my breath, and we sit down beneath the tall arch with its red posts and golden painted dragons. Manchester always feels different on Saturday mornings and today is no exception. The buildings have this pixelated fuzz to them, the air feels gloopy, time slows down. It's mostly the effects of sleep deprivation.

Everything feels hyperpixelated in the snow.

I tilt my head back and stare up at the Chinese arch, my mouth catching stray snowflakes that melt on my tongue. Stars cloud the edge of my vision, and I briefly wonder if Lucy drugged me. But I don't care. We're safe. For now at least.

A street cleaner whirs up and down the road. It must be like six in the morning now. We leave Chinatown, walk toward a greasy spoon café and push our way inside, the doorbell jingling as we enter. I hug Sabeena. "You should eat something. You look pale. Like proper ill-pale."

Sabeena nods. I order us strawberry milkshakes and a burger for myself.

We sit down at a white Formica table. The saccharine scent wakes me up. "What the fuck happened to us last night," I say, staring at Sabeena, then outside. My brain is scrambled, and I'm on edge, as if caught in a glitchy computer program. A mixture of feelings rip around my body—freedom, excitement, despair, guilt... and dread.

I push all those feelings aside.

The greasy stench of burger and gherkins hangs in my nose. I can't hold back anymore. I have to vomit. I run to the café toilet and retch. But I'm not sure we're out of danger yet.

"Take me through it," I say, sitting back down at the Formica table. What happened when you left me?"

Sabeena tenses. "I can't remember anything except Lucy giving me the headphones and then… black." She straightens up in her seat. "Do you think Lucy will follow us, that she knows where we are?"

A fuzzy sensation ripples along the back of my neck, like little jolts of electricity. I hesitate. "Not sure. We should move on. My mate works at the bead shop in Afflecks. There's a back room where we can hang out. We'll be safe there."

"Here." Sabeena presents me with the milkshake I've barely touched. "You should drink this. You need the energy."

I nod, reluctant, and take a loud slurp. We leave the café and sprint toward Afflecks, the alternative market we never steal from. When we reach Piccadilly Gardens, I freeze.

"What's that," I say, pointing to the distance.

On the horizon, black Tetris blocks appear from nothing, tall skyscrapers growing taller by themselves; no builders, no parachutes, no cranes. That is… impossible. I look up at the pixelated skyscraper growing taller by the minute in the distance, as light gusts of snow curl and blow across my vision.

A flash of lightning.

Thundersnow? No. That's not lightning. It's strobe. Acidic milkshake tugs at my throat. And then I remember the words Lucy said: *These young people, they all have a creativity we can use to rebuild the city.*

"Freeze." A voice shouts. "Return to scene one."

The world around us stops moving and then vanishes to gray.

I blink.

And we're back in the fourth room.

Trapped.

A.J. Hodges is a fiction writer, editor, and literary translator. They love writing speculative fiction with a touch of horror, otherworldly weird, or romance but cannot always promise a happy ending. Their literary translations have been published by Asymptote Journal and their fiction won an honorable mention in Foofaraw's An Ordinary Contest. Andy lives in a village outside Edinburgh, Scotland, where they enjoy trail running and mushroom foraging. Visit their website at: https://www.secondworldeditorial.com/andy-j-hodges

How To Paint a Prairie Ghost Train
by Tyler Lee

"Theron says we should paint the ghost train."

The words spin out of Gabe's crowded lungs like smoky spider-silk—faint, impossible threads hanging in the air. All but imperceptible until you walk into them. I mash the pause button on my controller and turn toward Gabe, Yoshi's kart frozen mid-drift on the flickering TV.

"Wait, *what?*"

Gabe cranes his neck and exhales a web of bong smoke into the unfinished basement ceiling, wisps twisting around exposed pipes, jittery aluminum ducts, splinter-ridden crossbeams. The haze drapes itself around the bare light bulb, bending the white rays an almost gunmetal grey. Gabe hacks like a cowboy about to die in an old Western, then clears his throat with a garden shovel and work gloves.

"Theron, that new kid. The big-ass twelfth grader from Hamilton," Gabe says, the silk-threads of his voice now wrapped in blood and sinew again. "I told him we tag. He says we should paint the ghost train. Like a big end-to-end, all three of us."

Gabe pulls the stem from the bong, and taps it out against the ashtray like Morse code. The tape deck on the shelf clicks as it hits the end of the cassette, then spins back to life as it flips sides and reverses direction. Xzibit's gravel voice growls through the speakers.

"What do you think?" Gabe asks.

"How the fuck are we supposed to piece the ghost train, Gabe?"

"Fucked if I know. We were skating on Main, and he brought it up. Figures we can do it, though, somehow. You going to school tomorrow? Could ask him about it."

The Vancouver Grizzlies poster on the front wall shakes harder—too hard to be caused by the speakers—plastic frame rattling against the particleboard walls. Two spears of white light slice in through the storm windows, broad blades dancing off the aluminum ducts, softening in the lingering smoke. I bounce from the sagging, corduroy couch, dart over to the entertainment stand, and ratchet the volume dial all the way down, revealing the rumble of a semi-truck idling in the front drive.

"Fuck, fuck, fuck." I scoop a can of aerosol air freshener from under my bed and pin the button down so hard the tip of my index finger tingles and turns red. The can hisses copperhead tongues as my body spins and pinballs, submerging the basement in a thick blanket of Pine Barren Petrichor or Spring Sunrise Redolence or what-the-fuck-ever IGA had on special this week.

"Bro, why is your dad home?" Gabe asks. "I thought you said he was on a long-haul?"

"He is. Wasn't supposed to be home until Monday night."

"Uhh, Jake—it *is* Monday night."

I have a math test on Monday—*had*, a math test—double-fuck. "Gabe, could you help out at least? I'm about to be in serious shit here." Gabe picks the bong off the coffee table and carries it to the far corner—behind the stairwell, next to the washer and dryer—then empties the water into the rusty iron floor drain. He retrieves a shoebox from under the couch—a battered-and-creased brown-and-orange Nike box, papered with skate stickers and Sharpie tags—tucks the bong, stem, and ashtray inside, and then slides the box back under the couch.

"Jake," Gabe says—voice like lake ice in early April—"I think I might clear out... It's just, your dad is kind of... You get it, right?"

"Yeah, don't worry about it bro. All good. Before you go, how does it smell in here now?"

Gabe inhales a cubic kilometer of aerosol perfume and sputters out a cough. "Uhh, smells like an anti-depressant commercial threw up in our Home Ec room."

I curl a smile. Gabe's eyes flash like a panther sniffing splashy, iron-rich blood on the breeze. "Smells like all the world's funeral flowers on the day disco died."

Laughter cracks out of me like embers floating up from a dying campfire. "That doesn't even make sense, dude."

Gabe turns his head, closes his eyes, and breathes in again. "It smells like a summer sleepaway camp where the counsellors make the kids braid friendship bracelets at gunpoint."

The campfire erupts—detonates, really. In between laughs, my lungs claw at the sky to regain their balance, dizzy-drunk on a cocktail of stale smoke, synthetic springtime, and domesticated basement dust. Gabe stares at me, "What? What's so funny?" his mock-Pesci pupil-twitch vibrates his blazed-red sclerae, a micron-thick layer of laughter-tears clinging like skin to his eyeballs. It all makes me think of simmering cream of tomato soup.

Then, the cold rattle of a brass doorknob, coffin-creak of steel hinges. A chill breeze flows down the stairs, floods into the room, extinguishes our hearth. Any lingering crackle of light or laughter turns first-snowfall-silent. The quiet is only broken by my father, his voice tumbling down the staircase like shards of avalanche ice.

"Jake, upstairs. Now. I won't ask twice."

Gabe stares at me, eyes still wet, but now frosted over. "It's okay," I say, "take off through the side door after I go up. I'll see you at school tomorrow."

"Yeah," Gabe says, "school tomorrow. Cool."

*

I'm at school an hour before first bell, face down in my black book at a cafeteria table, silver Sharpie in hand. My fingers won't follow my eyes, though. Skin tough and red from the ride to school, from holding my handlebars stiff against highway winds and truck-kicked gravel, knuckles and fingertips still tingling with the October morning cold. The marker tip doesn't glide today, it wobbles—film-reel judders along every line edge. A rat bastard's broken polygraph. I hear Gabe and Theron behind me, talking as they approach the table.

"Jakey, figured you were cutting again today. I heard Gabe clued you in to the idea," Theron says, sliding a plastic chair out from under the table and sitting down. "Madman stuff, just imagine it—Jesus Christ bro, what the hell happened to you?"

Theron locks both his eyes on just my left one—deep purple and swollen half-shut. He stares at me like I'm a half-developed Polaroid. "It's no big deal," I say, "I just racked out on my board last night."

Gabe looks at me, then Theron, then back at me. "Yeah, it was crazy bro," Gabe says, "you should have seen it. Jake ollied that four-set at the post office. Almost landed it, too, but then he went face-first into the planter box." Thank you, Gabe.

"Badass," Theron says. "You okay?"

I shrug my shoulders. "Been through worse." I had.

"Alright, well, try to keep all your limbs attached, you're going to need them when we piece the ghost train."

There's a vacant lot a little ways out of Chapel Head—the town we live in—where the old Saskatchewan Wheat Pool elevator used to be. The rest of the train line's been ripped out for years now, but for some reason there's still eighty or so meters of track in the ground there, weeds and prairie grass swallowing it back into the dirt. Every Wednesday night, a ghost train moves across that stretch of track. Engine first, then freights, caboose—just flickers into existence at one end of the track, flickers out at the other. A couple cars at a time, like watching a movie through a keyhole.

I flip my sketchbook shut and bury my tender hands in the front pocket of my paint-stained bunnyhug. "How are we supposed to tag a ghost train, Theron? It's a *ghost* train—it's right there in the name."

"I was out there last week," Theron says, "and the thing is, I pitched a bunch of rocks at it while it rolled past, and they clanked right off the side. Chucked an empty Pil bottle at it, and it smashed. Might be all glowing and spectral-looking or whatever, but that son-bitch is solid metal. Paint'll stick to metal."

The cafeteria gradually fills up. Some of the hockey-hairs and wrangler-shirts eyeball my swollen face, smirking in my peripheral, laughing at the precise edge of earshot. "Alright, so the train is real, but we still can't piece it, because it doesn't fucking stop. How fast do you think we paint?"

Gabe pipes up. "Okay, well do you remember Michelle? Corey Henderson's cousin from the city?"

"That goth chick who threw up Fireball and Fresca all over you at the lake back in August?"

"Bro, she's not a 'goth chick,' she's a straight-up, no-bullshit witch. She's got potions and crystals—"

"You mean rocks?"

"Crystals, and tomes—"

"Books?"

"Dude, just shut up for like five seconds, please. I'm telling you—she knows her stuff."

I shrug my shoulders and tilt my head down apologetically. "Sorry, I'll stop."

"Anyway… after I went home last night, I was thinking about the train again. I brought 'Chelle to check it out back in the summer and she said something cool. She said ghosts usually haunt places, right? Like Katie's great grandma at the old diner, Mr. Smith at the baseball diamond, that guy who plays banjo at the old dance hall. They're stuck—fixed—like a tree. Rooted to the ground. They can't leave where they're at because something holds them there, some kind of purpose. That's why the train is weird—a ghost that never stops moving. What's its purpose?"

The cafeteria noise grows—broken snippets of conversation, shoes squeaking on linoleum. A flinch snaps through my body as an empty, balled-up Doritos bag—Cool Ranch, by the look of it—flies past my shoulder, skips across our table-top, and tumbles to the floor, eliciting a round of deep, clustered laughter from somewhere behind me. Theron stabs a glance in the direction of the noise, and the laughter quickly subsides.

"Holy shit," I say, "I actually might have an idea."

My earlobes shiver as the bell rings. I gather up my books and zip them into my bag as we talk. "Theron, do you have your truck here today?"

"Damn straight, yup."

The Principal glares lasers at us through his horn-rimmed glasses. "Alright, let's meet up out front after school."

*

The "No Trespassing" sign is sun-faded, fence posts splintered and split, chicken-wire rusted from years of rain. I squeeze the bolt cutters, and the gate chain splits with a cracking noise, the padlocked end falling to the ground, kicking up a whirl of dust. I lead the truck up a rough, dirt path, overgrown with prairie grass, past a decaying farmhouse with boarded windows, a rusting tractor, and the footprint of a collapsed barn. After a careful descent down rough terrain—the hint of depth that passes for a valley in central Saskatchewan—I signal Theron to stop the engine at the edge of my grandfather's jungle—a dense grove of impossibly tall, twisted trees, thick brush, mosquitoes, and shadows. Theron and Gabe climb out of the truck.

"You sure we won't get in trouble?" Gabe asks.

"Nah," I reply. "We're far enough from the highway that no one will see us, and nobody in the family's been out here since grandpa died. Eight years now, I guess."

"Alright Jakey, what are we doing out here?" Theron asks.

I lead the group into the dimness of the woods. "Don't laugh at me, but when I was a kid, I was scared of ghosts— like, *really* scared of them. There weren't so many around back then, you know? I wasn't used to it."

On our right, we pass a faded blue telephone booth leaning against the trunk of a tree. A branch stretched through the booth's windows, and a bird's nest sits, weight balanced between the rough bark of the branch and the cold, black steel of the phone box. A steel-wrapped cord dangles from the phone, but the receiver has been chewed off by some kind of animal. The hint of a ringing sound lingers in the air.

"My dad used to bring me up here a lot when I was little. Grandpa was already circling the drain by then, but he wouldn't move to town. I can remember them arguing about it sometimes. Grandpa was a weird guy. Didn't like throwing things away, didn't like anything to go to waste. Said the world was getting wasteful—disposable. Stitch the pants, scrape the plate—typical old guy stuff, I guess, but he was…" I notice Theron looking at me. "It was just a big deal for him, that's all."

We walk past a pile of typewriters—scuffed vinyl shrouds on some, carriages exposed and rusting on others, some keys broken off, the symbols on others erased by wind, rain, and time. A gust knocks an acorn from an overhanging tree. As the acorn skitters down, rolling across the typewriters, their keys all swing into possessed motion. For a split-second, the jungle sounds like an old-fashioned press bullpen, typing blank memorandum at machine-gun speed.

"The farm scared the shit out of me. It's not so much the ghosts—there were a couple ghosts out here back then, but not nearly as many as you'd think—it was more like…" a half-dozen glass milk bottles dangling from twine in a nearby tree jangle in the wind, cascading rays of refracted light across the ground. "Okay, Gabe—you remember that spring a couple years back where the school gym flooded and they had to dig the floors out and replace them?"

"Do I remember it? My jump shot still hasn't recovered." Gabe scoops a pinecone off the dirt, jab-steps, and then launches it toward a nearby gramophone lying in the dirt. The pinecone bounces off the edge of the brass horn; a few seconds of distorted jazz piano plays. Gabe flings his arms to the sky in a fit of mock-despair.

"Well, you remember how they moved the assemblies to the choir room while they fixed the gym? And it was crowded, and stuffy, and it took forever to get everyone in through that one little door?"

"And it was hot as balls!" Gabe sings in an exaggerated falsetto, stretching the last note out like a manic Mariah Carey.

"My class was right next to the choir room, so we had to go in first every week. As bad as it was when the room was full-up—sweaty, sticky, just sitting and stewing and inhaling everyone's exhale—I swear to god it was worse when you first got in there, and the place was still empty. Worse sitting in the back corner, watching people filter their way in. Knowing that you can't leave—there's no way out, nowhere to go—and there's still more coming."

An old ox-wagon lies on its side, two wooden wheels buried deep in moss and dirt, the other two spinning rapidly, creaking against the axle. A grey field cat sleeps in the shade of the wagon's cargo box. "Being at the farm was kind of like that, I guess. It wasn't so much the ghosts who were up here, it was knowing how many more were on their way. I guess that's everywhere, but I felt it more out here."

We walk for a while in silence. We pass totems made of old wheat scythes, bound together by rawhide, with moss climbing their handles from the forest floor. Saskatoon trees growing out of empty ammunition crates like planter boxes, berries littering the ground around them, painting the earth purple. A receiving line of wooden mannequins dressed in olive drab army surplus. The rusting frame of a '40s Chrysler—wheels missing—with a tattered miniature Union Jack clinging to the radio antenna.

"I tried to run away one night and got lost in the woods."

"You tried to run away? Why?" Theron's voice pulls me back to my body—reminds me that he's still here. I glance at him, then back at Gabe.

"Yeah, you know..." I stammer a little. I remember my sketchbook this morning—pen won't follow my eyes; fingers won't follow my brain. A bird calls in the distance and a gust rustles the leaves. I breathe again.

"It's just my dad," I say, "sometimes he..." my head tips forward, my voice rolls up my windpipe, falls through my jaw, and lands on the ground. The moss sucks it beneath, swallows it to the pit of the earth.

Theron rests one of his enormous hands on my shoulder. "Hey, don't sweat it, Jakey. Parents fucking suck." Even through my bunnyhug, his palm feels warm. The corner of my left eye tickles like a butterfly wing, but I rub it away with my index finger. Theron takes his hand back and steps a few feet away.

"Right, yeah," I gather myself and speed up my pace, "fuck parents."

"Fuck parents!" Gabe sings at the top of his lungs.

"I got lost in the woods, and it was getting darker out—pitch-black, almost. But then I saw light through the trees. Like a glowing blue light, out of nowhere."

"Like the train," says Theron.

"Yeah, *just* like the train. I was scared as fuck. But I didn't know where else to go. So I followed the light, and it led me to this." We round a thicket of brush and enter a slight clearing—a gap in the canopy wide enough to let sunlight through. The clearing is littered with piles of salvage wood —planks, beams, boards—most of them the same dirty-clay-red as the hundreds of abandoned barns and farmhouses around here. A few dots of grey can be made out in the red—fragments of letters, shapes, symbols.

"Wait, is this..." Gabe trails off as he asks the question.

"Yup, and that night, it was all glowing."

It takes us the rest of the day and four trips in Theron's truck. Digging through the planks, finding the right pieces, lugging them down the dark, sinuous trails through the forest. We unload the boards near the train track, hiding them in a dried-out ditch. On the last trip, we stop by the school, and I pick up my bike, lofting it on top of the boards in the back of Theron's truck. It's past midnight when we finish unloading.

"You sure you don't want a ride home?" Theron asks.

"Nah," I say, "I think I need the air."

I roll past my house slowly. My dad's rig is still in the drive. I pedal past the house, then to the end of the block. I turn left and then right, pulling to a stop at the ball diamond. I lock my bike to the backstop and climb down into the dugout, sprawling out on the cold bench with my book-bag tucked under my head. The ghost of Mr. Smith chants "hey batter batter, swing" from behind home plate, but I drift to sleep, his voice little more than crickets.

School spins past at a chipmunk-fast-forward. After, we drive four towns out to the closest Peavey Mart for paint, and then suck back some fries and drumsticks from Chester's on the ride home—Theron's treat—launching our stripped-bare bones out the window like missiles aimed at the kelly-green marker signs that dot the highway ditches. By the time we pick up Theron's ladders, pull up to the train tracks, and drop the tailgate, the sun is already groundhog-digging down into the dusty horizon, and the October sky drips with the juice of bleeding wild berries.

"God damn." Theron somehow speaks and whistles with the same breath. "Won't lie, when Gabe told me you boys tag, I was shocked. Way out here in the middle-of-nowhere? Like, why?"

"And now?" I ask.

"Now I'm surprised anyone lives out here *without* painting."

From there, it's just a jigsaw puzzle. We drag the planks out of the ditch and start slotting them together—rough, battered edges, faded paint, splintered, and weathered. Our hands guide the work as much as our eyes do—palms finding corresponding grains and knots, fingers returning parts to a whole. The last streaks of colour leak out of the sky, but the Hunter's moon hangs high, raining down arrows of perfect moonlight. Theron moves the truck a few times to keep the headlights on our work and, before long, the shape materializes. Weathered red boards in a flat plane, lined up on the ground. Not nearly a building, sure, but something much more than a sketch of one, too. Near the top, a few massive lines of white-grey print. Softly sloping, rounded letters, all capitals:

SASKATCHEWAN

POOL

ELEVATORS

NO.725

CHAPEL HEAD

We retreat to the other side of the tracks, Theron moving the truck to cast the headlights on our canvas. I feel the ghost train before I hear it, and I hear it before I see it—fine gravel and packed dirt twitching under my Chuck Taylor soles, then iron scraping iron, rails flexing between wheel and earth. The train flickers into existence, a luminous blue-and-white aura wrapping black, burgundy, and rust-brown iron. A tower of light climbs from our jigsaw-slab of salvage wood—volume, shape, dimension. The train slows, then stops. To our right and left, the track edges divide a pair of freight cars—half oil-and-metal, half cold October air—but in the middle, in front of us, sits a complete tanker car.

Theron takes the front third. He tags the name "THOR," his caps barely containing the electricity in his barbarian hands, streams arcing like lightning from his sharp lines, letters twisting back around themselves like melting circuits. In the middle third, Gabe paints "GABE" because GABE is Gabe, and could never—*should* never—be anything else for an instant. Gabe paints with soup cans; warm and nourishing shapes, rotund bubble letters, like a liquid that expands to fill any bowl. I paint the back third. I used to paint "HERE" like frozen links of padlock chain—precise, geometric, unyielding. Tonight, I paint "GONE" like switchgrass and sunsets. Tonight, I paint without outlines, the colours and shapes blurring and bleeding into one another, a landscape seen through squinting eyes. Cans hiss and rattle, metal scrapes metal as we shift our ladders against the train car. Then, we finish.

Theron and I load the ladders and the rest of the paint back in the truck while Gabe snaps pictures, each flash punctuated by the clicking noise of advancing film. The train starts moving and then flickers out of existence, as the tower of light fades back to midnight black. We drag the pieces of the elevator back into the ditch and Theron hides them under camouflage hunting nets.

"That was a hell of a piece, boys." Theron says.

"I'll make you guys copies when I get the film developed." Gabe says.

"That's okay," I say, "I don't need them."

I haul my bike out of Theron's truck and pedal home. My dad's rig is gone. I walk inside and find a note on the kitchen table: *Jake, got a haul for Thunder Bay. Back Saturday. Don't fuck anything up while I'm gone.*

I stumble down the stairs and toss a tape in the deck—the new Outkast album Gabe dubbed for me on a cassette that's been written and re-written a hundred times—then collapse into my bed. *Hold On Be Strong* plays: strings pluck, keys echo, and a distant, faded voice sings to me like a ghost through the speakers. The cassette reels rotate, clicking just a little bit at the same spot on every orbit.

The rhythm reminds me of a train on tracks, inching forward, slow but ceaseless.

Tyler Lee is a writer, poet, and hip-hop artist. His work has been accepted for publication in Radon Journal, Neon & Smoke, and spring. Tyler lives in Saskatoon, Canada, where he owns a completely normal amount of sneakers, and definitely isn't on a first-name basis with the staff of his neighbourhood burrito spot.

Of Iron & Oatmeal
by Michael Allen Rose

I'm not very happy about it, but I ate the oatmeal.

I got the job through my father, who was a high-falutin' military muckity-muck with too much pull, brass balls to match his medals, and far too much confidence in a son who would rather play with himself than with guns and knives. Each time he would throw me a football and it would hit me in the face—sending me crying into the house —a little piece of him fell off and died, squirming on the lawn. He bought me my first BB Gun at the tender age of six and took me out into the backyard to shoot at cans. I fired in earnest, missing the cans entirely for the duration of an entire load of BBs, finally hitting the neighbor's dog with the final shot. The dog yelped, sending me into a crying fit. Even as my father assured me that I had not killed the dog, I screamed and apologized to the gods. I felt worse than Hitler. I would not stop bawling until he took the BB gun from my outstretched hands and, muttering, retreated into the house.

As a teenager, things got worse. I became moody and turned inward. My father pounded on the wall, trying to compete with my Bauhaus and Sisters of Mercy records. He bought me army green t-shirts, I scrawled messages on them in black Sharpie. I was too lazy or stoned to check my spelling, which meant that I often went to school with messages like "I only do whut the vices on my head teel me to." You can imagine my popularity level soaring through the roof like a balloon made of pig shit.

My father tried to make me call him "sir," but instead I started referring to him as "The General," which he absolutely despised. "That's incorrect! You know damn well

I'm a colonel!" He'd ground me. I'd sneak out. He'd get some poor sucker to watch me. I'd befriend my guard and take them out partying. But, despite this acrimony, we both survived, and my father, to his credit, just kept shaking his head and pushing. He was practically a modern-day Sisyphus. When I graduated high school (with straight C's), I was ready for a life of hanging out in the basement, working part-time at a record store, and trying to score pot from hippie chicks without standards. This, however, was not to be: in a last-minute Hail Mary play, my father shot and scored at the buzzer, landing me a "job opportunity."

"Son?" he asked, barging through the door of my room, "I'm coming in."

"You're already in," I muttered.

"Get up. Come on. You've got a job interview this afternoon." He stood stick-straight, years of military service having fused his spine into attention.

"But I—" I sputtered, before being manhandled out of bed and unceremoniously dumped into a suit jacket and shoved toward the dresser.

"Don't worry. It's civilian. You're not being forcibly enlisted."

"Are you sure?" I asked, removing the jacket so I could put on something resembling clothes. "A group of dudes with papers and handcuffs aren't about to jump me and make me sign things?"

"They won't allow that," said the General, unconvincingly.

As we drove, I tried to ask questions: "What's going on?" "What kind of job?" "Why are you doing this?" "Do you have any prescription medication? I have a headache." and the like. Silence was my only answer until we pulled onto the base. The guard saw the sticker on my dad's car, saluted, and we blew through the gates. I had been on the base before—a couple of times—and it always made me feel weird. I was no terrorist, but I always felt like I was waiting for some soldier to see the inside of my head, assume I was some kind of communist, and shoot me. I was glad that, despite being a military family, mom insisted we live off base and do our best to fit into townie culture.

We pulled up in front of a large, white three-story building on the east side of the base. I had never seen it before. There was a sign on the well-manicured front lawn, with large brown block letters that read: "LAUBER MILITARY TESTING INSTITUTE." I convulsed, a symptom of what I called "mild tourette's" and what the doctors called "general anxiety about life."

"Go ahead," dad commanded, "Doctor High is waiting for you."

I snickered, and he cuffed the back of my head, causing my vision to flicker.

"Listen, do what they tell you, and do good work," he said.

"When do I get picked up?" I started to ask.

He leaned over and opened the passenger side door, shoving me out unceremoniously. "They pay weekly. Have fun and do what they tell you."

Before I could mutter my distaste, the car was already halfway down the street and turning the corner.

Receptionists can go one of two ways, stereotypically speaking. One, they can be frumpy, no-nonsense, and a little scary. Alternately, they can be sexy and delightful, like a sweet song floating on the breeze. The receptionist at the Lauber Military Testing Institute was the rare combination of both at once.

The lobby was decorated with 1970's furniture, a wash of wooden paneling, and comfortable looking couches. A pristine, gleaming white desk, looking far too modern for the room, stood imposingly opposite the front doors. Behind the desk, a young woman sat typing something into a computer. She was a redhead, the waves of her hair cascading like seawater across the shore of her shoulders. I looked her over and her plunging neckline revealed the edges of large, full breasts, with just a tiny slip of light blue lace showing beyond the collar of a maroon dress. She looked like a model, not a military receptionist.

Shyly, I approached the desk, unsure of what to say. I stood there, dumbly for a minute, listening to the clicking of her keys. Finally, I cleared my throat.

"Fill out the form, bring it back up here when you're done," she said, never looking up. Her hand left the keys long enough to pull a clipboard from behind the desk and push it across to me with ruthless efficiency.

"I'm here for a job?" I said, hesitantly, "My father is—"

"Fill out the form, bring it back up here when you're done," she said, louder this time, still focused on the screen in front of her.

I took the clipboard from her, wordlessly, and took a seat on one of the ratty orange and brown patterned love-seats. Dad hadn't said anything about filling out forms—I had assumed this was a done deal, whatever it was. The form was long and detailed, and became more than a little confusing as it went on:

Name: Robert Patton McKinley.

Age: Nineteen.

Are you now, or have you ever been a member of the Captain Video Telephone Fun Club? No. I don't know what that is, and I was born after landlines went extinct. And video, for that matter.

It was generally pretty easy until I got to questions like boiling point, facial symmetry ratio, and weight of edible meat contained in physical form. Drawing on the methods

I'd perfected in high school, I sketched some duckies with machine guns in lieu of writing things down. Perfect.

The hot lady receptionist didn't say much when I handed her the clipboard back. I watched her eyes scan it over without much interest, then she shrugged and pointed to her right. "Through the doors, to your right. Have a seat in there, and you'll be called when it's your turn. Bathrooms are to the left. Don't drink or eat anything until after your interview. Thank you."

"What am I applying for?" I stood there, blinking. She squinted at me, looking me over from head to toe, and decided something, as her eyes went off like flashbulbs and she sighed with heavy theatricality.

"Follow me." The receptionist walked me through the double doors and into a huge rectangular space, cubicles receding into the distance and blurring into a soupy stew of noise and motion somewhere on the horizon. The walls were enormous, spattered with giant motivational posters, as big as unrolled elephant skins. It reminded me of a barn, only instead of animal shit, it smelled like coffee and artificial fruit with an undercurrent of nervous sweat.

"This is a call center? Is this a phone job? I thought it was a Military Testing Institute."

She chewed her gum briskly, her eyes narrowing. "It is. It's lots of things." The gum snapped like a gunshot and something inside me convulsed like an angry hiccup. "Just follow the guidelines and you'll be fine."

The calling floor was swarming with people, men and women, all wearing little red and white name tags. Before I could ask any further questions, the receptionist vanished, and I was left alone at the mouth of this bustling hive of activity. A portly man with too many teeth grinned his way toward me. His smile looked permanently etched into his skull, like a scar. A frown would look unnaturally artificial on this man's face, unsettling like cracking an egg for an omelette and finding a live baby alligator.

"Robert? Hi there, nice to meet you, I'm Barry."

The large man shook my hand, with a firm grip. I watched his arm fat jiggle as I found myself asking "How did you know my name?"

He ignored this. "Glad you came in. Very excited for your interview. Follow me. You find the place okay?" He strolled through the maze of cubes with purpose, as I jogged to keep up.

"My dad dropped me off."

"Good, good, here we go." We arrived at a small, undecorated office to the side of the large room. A table of dark, scarred wood lay in the center of the room. The walls were blank, no windows or doors besides the one came through, except for a rectangular metal portal on the side of the room. It was painted gray, with hinges and latches affixed to the corners. A small counter jutted out below. "Sit down, make yourself comfortable."

I sat in the chair nearest to me, allowing myself to plop down with authority. The castors squeaked. Meanwhile, Barry circumvented the table, passing near the metal port in the wall, and tapped on it three times with his knuckles.

Almost immediately, the latches popped open, and the hatch opened up. A pair of gloved hands pushed an orange cafeteria tray through the opening, and left it sitting on the counter. Barry picked up the tray and brought it over to the table, setting it in front of me, and taking his own seat.

It was a bowl filled with some kind of fresh, hot porridge. The aroma wafting from it reminded me of the country. It was a yellowish color, not quite off-white. Chunks of some unidentifiable substance broke the surface here and there like icebergs in a tiny sea. Fruit, maybe? A large spoon was arranged next to it, atop a napkin.

"What is this?" I asked.

"Oatmeal. So, can you tell me a little bit about your experience? Have you ever done phone work before? Customer service?"

"Oatmeal?"

"Yes. Is this your first phone job?"

"Yeah, I... haven't really done... why is there oatmeal?"

"Go ahead, just eat the oatmeal." I noticed he had the clipboard with the application I'd filled out earlier. I didn't remember seeing anyone hand it to him.

"How did you...?"

"It says on your application that you haven't really had too many regular jobs before. Other than the record store? Is that right?"

"I guess not, I mean, I've done freelance work for people, yard work, watching my friend's convenience store while he grabs a smoke. But I'm sure I can figure it out. I'm friendly. This can't be too much different from shooting the shit about music, can it?"

He laughed way too hard at this, an ear-shattering, donkey chortle. If he could, I feel like he'd have reached all the way across the table and curled his arm around me to smack my back.

"Yes, I'm sure you can handle it. There are scripts for all of this. You just follow the script, based on what the caller needs. Simple. Anyone can do it. Do you need cinnamon? Sugar?"

"What?"

"For the oatmeal."

I stared down at the still steaming bowl. "No?"

"Okay, well, everything seems to be in order. Go ahead and just eat the oatmeal, and we'll get you set up with a headset and a cube so you can start right away."

He folded his hands under his chin, leaning his fat head on his knuckles, and fluttered his eyelashes at me. Maybe because I was uncomfortable with Barry staring at me, I didn't know what else to do, so I reached down, grabbed the spoon, and pushed it down into the oatmeal. It enveloped the utensil like a boot in a swamp.

"I'm not really hungry. Can I... just...?" I didn't really know how to finish that question.

Barry frowned and stood up. He walked to the little metal door and knocked on it again. Immediately, it slid open, and two hands floated through the opening. They handed Barry two shakers, one marked "Brown Sugar" and the other marked "Cinnamon."

"Here. Dry additives only. Liquid changes the *efficacy*."

I took a long look before reaching out and grabbing the shakers. Upending them, I shook out a few granules of each, and gave the bowl a stir.

The first bite was pretty okay. It was bland, but not unappealing. I caught eyes with Barry and put another spoonful into my mouth. It didn't take long to finish the bowl. When I did, I felt the nervous energy suspended in the room leak out like air from a balloon.

"Good. You like softball? We have a softball team. Meets Thursdays." Barry practically pulled me to my feet and ushered me out of the room. "Take a fifteen minute break every four hours. Shifts of eight or more get you a half an hour lunch too. That's paid."

By this point, he was pulling me down a fluorescent corridor of cubicles. On every side of me, dozens, maybe hundreds of people buzzed like hornets in a hive, talking on headsets, clicking computers, poking tablets with their fingers, and generally creating a cacophony.

Before I could ask anything further, Barry pushed me gently down into a rolling chair. Before me, on the particleboard desktop surface, a plastic-wrapped headset and a bagged cordless mouse lay prostrate before a large monitor. The sound of a desktop computer whirring away quietly reached my ears from beneath the desk, before Barry spoke again.

"Follow the scripts. Here's your manual. I'll check on you in an hour or two."

A well-used photocopied booklet hit the desk in front of me, startling me. It was thick, and as I paged through it, I saw endless columns that all seemed to be cross-referenced with computer codes. Responses, replies, and scripts for every scenario. I wish I'd asked what we did here. I wish I'd asked where the bathroom was, as I held back a dribble of fear pee. What the hell was I supposed to do now? I moved the mouse inside its little baggie, and the screen blazed to life.

First name. Last name. Hit enter. A diagram of how to put on the headset properly, and then a whole litany of instructions. Step by step. Everything I needed to know, with hyperlinks and search term highlights.

It appeared this was a call center for a variety of different departments, which is why the instructions were so intricate. The book was divided into dozens of sections. I flipped through with my thumbs, and saw everything from "Tax Code Department" to "Hydrogen Bomb Victim Help Line" to "Area 52," calls to which were to be answered specifically: "Area 52, there is no Area 51, it doesn't exist, and it's one number less anyway, which makes it objectively worse. Please reply 'affirmative' if you've found the Voyager golden record and are extraterrestrial to planet Earth, otherwise hang up, check your number, and dial again."

I plugged my headset into the port, and instantly, a digital series of beeps sounded off. I clicked the "answer button" on my screen and words flashed across it like a karaoke machine. The display code read "OCR."

✶

"Office of Civilian Relations, this is Robert, how may I help you today?"

"Hello? Is this America?"

Her voice was small, a lick of some sandy foreign accent rolling around the edges of her consonants. I didn't feel nervous, but for some reason, I was sweating. I patted down my forehead with my free hand, and it came away moist and clammy. I wiped it on my jeans and continued.

"Yes ma'am, this is the Office of Civilian Relations," I nervously replied, scanning the screen and the book for responses and codes in a whirl of letters and numbers, "How may I... help you?"

"There are troops here on my farm. They are scaring my goats and making my children nervous."

I looked at my chart of handy responses, my finger tracing over the grimy, yellowing laminate protecting the paper until it came to rest beneath "Troops in yard/farm" in the "case" column. Subsection C under the row read "frightened/upset ungulates."

I input the code from the book on the screen, and immediately, a series of windows popped up with scripts, definitions, an FAQ, and several high-definition photographs of goats.

"I understand and I'd be happy to assist you. Where are you located?"

She spelled the name of her city for me, a place with consonant pairings I was unfamiliar with.

I noticed a blinking icon in the corner of my display. I clicked on it and a visible waveform showed up under a window entitled "full spectrum analysis." The computer was recording the call and responding to me and this woman in real time. Before I'd even finished typing in the name of the city, maps were opening, and the script highlighted some words and scrolled down.

"Is this Ms. Suri Ghorbani?"

A pause. "Yes."

"Excellent, I just need a little more information," I said, reading off the screen. The cursor blinked in another field with a neon green arrow.

"Okay, fine."

I had an odd thought, and needed to express it. "Do you speak any other languages besides English?"

The screen immediately flashed a bright red pop-up window that said "DO NOT IMPROVISE. STICK TO THE SCRIPT."

"I'm not speaking English. I'm speaking Farsi. What are you talking about?"

Did I somehow learn to speak Farsi without even trying? Was I some kind of savant?

"It's the translator," a strange, low, gravelly voice echoed in my ear.

"Excuse me?" I asked, wondering how the lady changed her voice so thoroughly.

"I said it was fine. What information do you need? My goats are freaking out."

I read a list of contact information queries from the screen, and Ms. Ghorbani quickly answered them. I could tell she was losing her patience. "Listen, I complained to one of the officers here, and they gave me a card with this number, and I need you do something. Have you ever tasted the milk of an upset goat? It's terrible."

In large, red, white, and blue letters, the screen kept spitting out responses.

"If you can hold on just one moment, ma'am, I'll take care of that for you." I stared at the screen. How was I supposed to take care of soldiers invading a farm on the other side of the planet? I figured maybe the system would tell me how to log a complaint for her, or at least have me read some kind of propaganda about America helping out in her area —with emphasis on gratitude and patriotism and such.

Suddenly, my guts started acting funny. It was like an attack of irritable bowel syndrome, with painful cramps and rumbling pockets of gas.

My guts were rolling and boiling. A low moan escaped my lips as I rubbed circles around my belly, trying to coerce my guts to cooperate. The pain was getting worse. I rotated the chair idly left and right as I swiveled my head, looking for anyone that seemed like a supervisor. Seeing nobody, I fought back a wave of nausea and struggled to get up, but when I tried to stand, I couldn't even get off the chair. I felt like my digestive system weighed a thousand pounds.

"Hello, are you still there?" asked Ms. Ghorbani.

"Yes, sorry—" I managed to grunt, as I doubled over. I reached for the headset, fearing I'd end up being sick and making a mess on my first day of work. I needed to find a restroom, stat.

Almost immediately, the computer flashed another red window, and that same voice from before, the low, gravelly one, appeared in my ear. "Don't remove the headset."

I felt a tickle rolling up my throat, like a long hair was stuck at the very back, irritating my uvula, making me simultaneously gag and cough. My tongue flattened to the bottom of my mouth, and I felt my cheeks puff up as bile began to rise and soak the back of my gums. I tried desperately to move the mouthpiece away from my face before I vomited all over it, but my arms disobeyed, keeping it pressed against my lips.

"Hello? Hello? Are you listening to me?" I heard the voice on the other end of the line becoming increasingly irritated.

Just then, something wet and bulbous forced its way into my mouth. I felt full, like I'd given birth to one of those novelty jawbreaker candies. The chunk of matter pulsed and pushed its way forward. Grimacing, my eyes closed instinctively to save myself the humiliation of barfing all over myself and my work station. With the sound of a particularly large turd hitting toilet water, the chewy mass scraped past my teeth and outward. I peered down at my mouthpiece, trying to keep myself grounded. It was fine, and no half-digested food was piled in my lap. I blinked a few times.

"Can I speak to your supervisor, please?" I'd almost forgotten about the person I was talking to in my brief moment of panic.

I tried out my mouth. All the muscles seemed to work as usual. "I'm sorry, ma'am, there was a momentary... crisis. Please, let's continue."

"I don't know what—" Her voice was cut off by a loud "schloomp." I imagined a watermelon being emptied of its contents with a particularly large plunger.

The screen opened a window displaying a large "10", and text underneath read: "Operator, please hold for the retrieval process."

The number changed to a "9". Then, an "8".

A sound came through the speaker. Like a hose being dragged through wet grass.

"Ms. Ghorbani?" There was no reply, but a pop-up window informed me that I should relax and silence any extraneous speech or utterance.

"7." I felt something vibrate. My mouth opened up slightly like I was about to go in for a kiss. I was not involved in this decision. "6." On "5" I felt something slide into my mouth. It was warm. I gagged a little. "4." I was practically paralyzed. I wondered if this is how coma victims feel? My senses still worked, but I was no longer in control of what I was doing. My brain simply wouldn't send the electrical impulses to my muscles. On "3" I heard "relax" in my mind's eye. Not audibly, not with my ears exactly, but with the part of my mind that processes hearing. I know that sounds weird, but it was like when you're hypnotized at one of those comedy shows where they make you think you're a turkey, or forget the number seven. Your brain knows none of it is real, but you're doing these things anyway, and you can't really understand why, and somehow, you don't really care.

"2." It's kind of like being on nitrous oxide. Part of your brain is there, but it's floating on an inflatable purple hippo in a swimming pool, not really giving a shit whether or not you're cognizant. The lump in my mouth slithered down my throat, and as I tried to gargle, a strange sense of calm came over me. My brain must have been firing shots of serotonin and dopamine into the air like a celebrating Texan. "1." "O.". The timer disappeared, and I sat back in my chair as a pop-up window declared the call successfully completed. I looked around, trying to peer into the other cubes to see how my colleagues were doing, but they were designed so that everyone was visually isolated. I clicked the "Break" button in the bottom right corner of the screen. Immediately, a 15-minute timer popped up and began counting down.

*

Nobody was in the breakroom when I found it. The vending machines stood against one wall, arranged like tombstones, with various generic names like "COFFEE," "SNACK," and "SODA" marking where junk food went to die. In the corner stood a larger machine, unmarked. A stack of wax-coated paper bowls towered next to it, along with a canister of individually wrapped plastic spoons. Behind the glass, a series of colored LED lights illuminated signs.

"Apple Cinnamon, Strawberry Cream, Maple Brown Sugar, Plain..." I read aloud.

"How's it going?" a loud voice startled me. I turned to see Barry, grinning that huge plastic grin, leaning against the door frame. "Break time, already?"

"I didn't feel well," I said.

Barry walked over to me and put a reassuring hand on my shoulder. It was cold and clammy. "You'll get used to the job. It takes a little time, but soon, you'll be in and out of calls like clockwork. Heck, I bet you'll be on the leaderboard in no time."

"I don't know. I think I'm sick. Maybe I should go home?"

"Nonsense, you just need a pick-me-up. Here, pick a flavor." His fingers hovered over the buttons on the colorful, wordless machine. With his free hand, he grabbed a bowl and slid it into an opening in the machine's front. "You like Raisin Walnut?"

"I don't think I want any more oatmeal right now. I don't know if that first bowl messed up my stomach or what."

"Trust me, this stuff is just the thing for stomach problems. Good, stick-to-your guts kind of stuff. Here, try this. Berries and cream. Personal favorite." He pressed a couple of buttons and the dark red LED light blinked a few times. A chute in the machine started pumping out hot, steaming oatmeal, and a few seconds later, Barry turned and presented it to me.

I looked down at it and then up at him. I took a bite. It was actually pretty good. The taste was bright and fruity. I thoughtfully chewed it and swallowed. As soon as I did, I heard my stomach gurgle, and without warning, patterns and lights started to flash before my eyes. My head went woozy and I stumbled, but before I fell over, a feeling of peace and tranquility flooded in and then, I felt better.

"Now, let's go back to your desk. Try another few calls. I'll be wandering the floor if you need me, but now that your stomach is full, I think you're going to be fine. Sometimes you just need a little refill."

Barry led me back to my cube, which showed just a few minutes left on the clock. I sat down and took a deep breath, glancing over my shoulder at Barry. His smile hadn't moved, but something in his eyes was different. Like, his mouth was smiling, but his eyes were doing something else entirely.

I put on the headset and sat, staring at the countdown. I had to admit, I was feeling better than earlier. The timer reached "0" and immediately, a call came in. I read my lines off the display.

"Office of Contamination and Isolation, how may I help you?"

"Yes... hello. I was told to call this number after being diagnosed with a virus?"

"Can you read me the code written on your intake slip?" A little purple box awaited my input.

"Sure. It's um... 3A7-C19?"

"Perfect, thank you. Your name, sir?"

"Todd Berryman. Do you need my insurance information or..?"

"One moment."

A map window appeared and I watched the system track the call in real time. Little by little, it zeroed in on an address, and I watched as a small arrow moved down the sidewalk from a sky-high view.

"How long have you been experiencing these symptoms?" I asked, prompted by the screen.

"About a week or so."

An overlay appeared—it looked like a heat map—and the little arrow turned dark red. "Please hold, sir." My stomach burbled again. Apparently, the oatmeal had done little to settle it. This time, there was no pain, just a lot of noise. I couldn't hold back a burp, and immediately felt my face turn red with embarrassment.

"Excuse me?" asked the man's voice on the other end of the line.

"Be still," said an entirely different, guttural voice. I wondered if he'd heard it too?

A tendril of something hit the back of my throat like I was upchucking a strand of uncooked spaghetti. My cheeks puffed outward and I made a weird noise like a rapidly deflating balloon. My lips parted and I felt something dribble over my gums. My eyes closed involuntarily and I hacked up a wad of phlegm. Still coughing, I panicked, crossing my eyes trying to look at the headset. Everything looked normal. I swallowed, trying to maintain normal breathing.

"What other information do you need?" the man asked. He coughed a few times, and then a sort of squishing sound came out of him. "Mmmfgh! Oh God, what's mmmfgh!" The beginning of a scream was cut short.

I listened to the silence on the other end of the line. "Hello? Mister Berryman?"

Once again, the screen began its ten second countdown, encouraging me to remain still for the retrieval process. This time, I tried to stand up, but my limbs didn't seem to be cooperating. My mouth began to open up. Frantically, I tried to take my headset off, but my arms wouldn't respond. "No... no... no!" I said, kicking and thrashing. My movements were too small, too weak. Why couldn't I move? It was like being stuck in slow motion in a nightmare. The countdown read "7..." "6..."

Shaking with effort, I managed to turn my chair so the headset cable wrapped around the arm. I felt something inside me tear as I wrenched my body to the side with enough force to unbalance me. The whole chair tipped over, with me attached. My head cracked into the floor, with only my shoulder saving me from a concussive blow. As I fell, the headset pulled free from my skull, still attached to the machine, and spooled around me like a long, black noodle.

I groaned, trying to control my shaking body, as the headset shuddered. On "3," something liquid began to seep out, followed on the count of "2" by a mass of gray goo. It was the oatmeal, or something derived from it. It didn't look digested; it looked alive. It piled up on the floor in a slimy, twitching glob, and began to emit a high-pitched scream. Pulling myself up on my elbows, I began to shuffle backwards, kicking at the pile, trying to stomp it down into the carpet.

"What the fuck are you? What is this?" I squealed, grinding the oatmeal into the floor. I retreated until my back hit the wall of the cubicle opposite mine, and sat there hyperventilating as the ooze began to vibrate. It appeared to be breathing, but my attack had broken it up into multiple dollops, many of which were curling up and turning black as I watched the thing die.

My nausea returned, and I gagged up a long string of bile. I was too weak to move, and just sort of leaned over and let it drip out of my gullet, a long, metallic string of grayish filth.

"Oh no, this is unfortunate." It was Barry's voice. I looked up, and saw multiple heads peeking out from their cubes all down the row. Some were shaking their heads, a few looked frightened, but they all had the same look of calm resolution deep within their eyes. Barry was standing with his arms folded, flanked by two men in red shirts wearing security badges.

"What—?" I managed, before being hauled to my feet by the two security guards.

"It's okay, it's not your fault. This happens." He looked down at the blackened lump that had sprung from the headset, lying still like scorched mashed potatoes. "That's too bad. Two servings wasted. Usually, that's enough for most people as a starter."

They ushered me down a hall to a small room, similar to the one I had interviewed in earlier. Was that the same day? It felt so distant now. They sat me down in what looked like a dentist's chair. I was too weak to resist and had to watch as they strapped me in. I was completely drained and could only turn my head. Barry's smile was still in place, but his features showed some concern. He was looking at me with sympathy for an animal that had been hit by a car, when the prognosis wasn't very good. I felt myself being lowered into a supine position.

"It doesn't always take right away. Something to do with the employee's metabolism. Maybe body chemistry. I keep telling them, we should start doing drug testing, see if marijuana intake affects the bonding process, but of course, they're afraid if we do that, we lose the stoners, which, as you can imagine, make up a hefty portion of our employee base." Barry chuckled as one of the red shirts wheeled over a cart with a large metal pot and some machines attached, whirring away quietly.

The other guard pulled the top off the pot and stirred its contents with a long, wooden spoon. The air filled with the unmistakable aroma of cinnamon.

Another figure appeared from the darkness, a woman, wearing a surgical mask and gown. "Please try to relax," she said. "I'm doctor High, and I'll be taking care of you today." I noticed that Barry had put on a mask as well, and he hovered over my face. I could imagine that smile beneath the cloth and it looked the same.

"What's happening? I don't want any more oatmeal!" I cried, slurring my words. I felt a quick prick in the arm. They must have injected me with something.

"Shhh, it's going to be all right. The oatmeal will heal you."

"What the hell is it?" I mumbled.

While lying there in shock, flat on my back, Doctor High placed an endoscope into my mouth and down my esophagus.

"Don't worry," said Barry in a soothing voice, "The camera helps the doctor visualize your stomach lining to ensure that the feeding tube is positioned properly."

I tried to sit up, to fight, to scream, but I was a mannequin.

"When the doctor can see your stomach, she is going to make a small incision in your abdomen. Next, she'll insert the feeding tube through the opening. Then, she'll secure the tube and place a sterile dressing around the site. Just FYI, there may be a little drainage of bodily fluids—such as blood or pus—from the wound, so we'll keep an eye on that. The whole thing will only take an hour or so. We'll be done before lunch." He patted the side of the large pot. "Although, I don't imagine you'll be very hungry."

My eyes pleaded with him, as I tried to speak around the endoscope. All that came out was "wffissttt."

"What is it? Oh, we don't know. Well, I don't know. That's way above my paygrade. Alien technology? Nanobots? A pact with demons? Some kind of virus?" He leaned in, conspiratorially. "Personally, I think it's a combination of all of them. I think the government made a deal with the devil, who provided some kind of tiny alien robot that spreads and replicates itself like a virus. All we know for sure is that it helps solve America's problems, and it makes for loyal and compliant employees."

Picture a swamp, bubbling with gaseous emissions of sulfur. That's what the oatmeal sounded like, as it pumped itself into the tube and began to fill my stomach cavity.

Later that day, I had taken a dozen new calls. Every single one of them successful. You get used to the process after a while. People say they can hear my smile when I talk to them on the phone. I think that's true. I just wish they could see what's behind my eyes.

Michael Allen Rose is an award-winning author, musician, and performer based in Chicagoland. His novel Jurassichrist won the Wonderland Award for best bizarro fiction of 2021, and in 2022 he received the Wonderland for best collection for his illustrated horror primer Last 5 Minutes Of The Human Race. Blending genres including horror, comedy, and bizarro fiction, Michael has been published in numerous anthologies such as Tales From The Crust, The Magazine of Bizarro Fiction, and Dragon Mythicana. He also runs a small press called RoShamBo Publishing, makes industrial music under the name Flood Damage, and is president of the national Bizarro Writers Association. He loves tea and cats.

Something Stirs
by T.K. Kestrel

Morning loosens from the treeline
  pale... and trembling... threadlike... thin.
I step forward where it wanders;
  something stirs and draws me in.

By the roots a shape is waiting,
  still as frost on shadowed stone.
Not a whisper marks its presence;
  only I can sense its own.

Soft its flank begins to quiver;
  soft its heartbeat stains the air.
I move closer, half in wonder,
  half in something rising there.

"I mean no harm," I tell the stillness
  strange how swift the words appear;
strange how hollow... how uncertain...
  how they tremble into fear.

For the path recalls this moment
  I have heard that sound before.
And the hush grows tight around me,
  tightening like a closing door.

Then the creature snaps to motion
  sudden spark of frantic flight.
In its wake, my blood awakens,
  burning... cold, and burning bright.

My feet forget their measured choosing;
  path and pulse break out of time.
Something claws against my pacing;
  then the question snaps alive.

A whisper stirs the branches:
  Each one flees the same old way.
All their terror, all their trembling
  echoes from a farther day.

All their fear becomes a pattern
  I have heard that sound before.
Now the truth crowds at the threshold,
  knuckles white upon the door.

Still I linger, breath uncertain,
  watching where the fleet shape ran.
All are hunted when they wander
  prey to path... or prey to plan.

Something older keeps my cadence;
  something waits where choices end.
And the morning, dim and listening,
  threads my shadow through its dread.

T.K. Kestrel is a poet from Chicago who enjoys words being horizontal..

Annotated Draft Menu, Winter 2025 Prix-Fixe
by Andrea Cavedo

[GM's note: No prices are fixed right now. Eggs are still changing hour to hour. Do not call attention to this. "Winter 2025 Gustation" maybe?]

*

Appetizer

nettle orechiette, date, goat cheese, saba

carmelized beets, whipped ricotta, coffee reduction

[Solid twist on a classic. But with the 10% blanket tariff on coffee and additional 50% on Brazilian beans, sub chicory here, or maybe molasses.]

toasted enriched yeast roll, artisan curd, Maldon

[This is just bread and butter, right? Nice.]

*

Main

bourguignon, cipollini, melted parsnip, crouton

[Great job not naming the protein here – could be beef, could be an Impossible burger. Could be the chickpeas we bought in bulk before the tariffs started and now we can't seem to move. Don't say that though, obviously. "Chef's choice."]

chicken, scratch dumpling, Jerusalem artichokes, squish broth

[Really liking the nostalgia here, but it's too political—call them "sunchokes" at least. And squish? You mean squash, I hope, because remember, we over-bought kabochas a few weeks back when we thought prices were trending down and could really use that walk-in space now.]

garlicky starchy rice-y risotto with spicy cheesy ricotta whip, crispy frizzly shallots

[Now you're just messing with me.]

Side

lemony cabbage
cabbagey lemon
fries

[Guys. Come on.]

Dessert

ooey gooey soupy gluey choco slice - gluten-free

[What the actual fuck. This tasting menu costs $255 plus included 18% gratuity plus secret table service fee. Our job is comfort and escape, remember? Taking everyone's mind off the news for a few hours? "Flourless chocolate cake" is fine, it's retro.]

*

passionfruit ICE melt, watermelon gelee, rainbow sorbetto quenelle

[Jesus Christ, you guys are killing me. I know what you're going for here. Believe me, I'd love to call it "Essence of the last days of summer catching lightning bugs in fruit-sticky hands under the big elms, when the ice pop melted on your tongue with the perfect sweetness of your own innocence, before masked January 6 parolees ran off all the paleteros and half our kitchen staff, and the city closed the park because of the homeless encampments, and you stopped going outside—except for very special occasions—because of the violence on the train and the teargas on your street, and you were forced to look at your dwindling savings account and face the certainty of the long and painful winter ahead." But we can't. How about "off-season sorbet"?]

tears of your enemies, revenge, chilled

[Okay, fine. It's about the only thing that sounds good right now, anyway. Chef's choice.]

Andrea Cavedo's writing has appeared in McSweeney's, Chestnut Review, HAD, and others; she won Foofaraw's inaugural Ordinary Contest, and has been a semifinalist for The Sewanee Review's Fiction, Poetry & Nonfiction Contest. For the last decade she has taught history and government to Chicago high school students.

Find her online at www.andreacavedo.com.

A review of "(Skin)" by Chelsea Sutton, published in Diabolical Plots
by Vito Guffa

There are plenty of short stories that center on miracles, but few stories feel like actual miracles themselves. And that's true of Chelsea Sutton's "(Skin)," published in *Diabolical Plots* in October 2025.

In "(Skin)," Sutton, a self-described writer of "gothic whimsy," does something remarkable: not only does she juggle a novel's worth of points of view over the course of 3,000 words, but she manages to wrap up a bizarre fable in a bold and experimental style. It should be too much for so few words (or even one writer), but Sutton pulls it off gracefully.

"(Skin)" tells the story of Estelle Irby (or more precisely Irby's skin). In the opening lines, Irby passes away at home in front of her wife, daughter, and doctor. But when the last breath leaves Irby's body, something strange happens. Like a soul rising up to heaven, her skin peels away from her body and starts walking around. While Irby's wife and daughter grieve and recall those special, private moments with Irby, the doctor sees an opportunity. Recognizing this as the scientific discovery of a lifetime, the doctor—who has no interest in the miracle's meaning or usefulness—believes it can make him very rich. Before the skin can be restrained, he's already lining up buyers for portions of Estelle Irby's sentient skin. Of course, it all ends up very bad for the (good) doctor, and the story's conclusion brings us back to the family at the center of it all in a satisfying and emotional final paragraph.

What's most striking throughout "(Skin)" is Sutton's use of parentheticals. What might be a gimmick in a lesser writer's hands becomes an integral part of the story's style and form. This choice infects nearly every line, including its title, and Sutton lets this choice communicate so much of what cannot be said. The parallels between the mark of punctuation and the central metaphor of skin are obvious: both serve as a boundary, a fence designed to enclose. Yet what we find inside those parentheticals is as varied as the various plot threads woven into the story. Sutton manages to include moments of tenderness ("clicking and puckering her mouth in all sorts of strange sounds meant to withhold Estelle's true (always proud, always warm) feelings"), cynicism ("Dr. Rannow made a list of the many ways he could retire on this discovery (the whole business of dying was tedious, boring, and certainly he couldn't spend another thirty years doing this)"), and humor ("The nurse, oblivious to what was happening with the Skin (though knowing Estelle Irby was bound to expire any minute, and hoping it would be soon, as she had a pre-paid Zumba class to go to that evening and did not want to lose that $30), was a bit confused"). The language throughout is beautiful and precise, made up of the kind of winding sentence structures expected from a 19th-century novelist, but Sutton's use of parentheticals makes the journey to each full stop feel like an innovative (and modern) voyage rather than a struggle.

And while the overall story coheres well, there might be a bit of sag in the middle as we take an extended detour, following the (good) doctor's capitalistic pursuits. The writing, unsurprisingly, is consistently brilliant, but the doctor subplot, though it provides for an interesting contrast in perspective, might distract from the story's emotional core, which centers Irby's wife and daughter and their shared (and unshared) grief.

Nonetheless, I think it's a story that demands reading. Sutton somehow crams "(Skin)" full of chaos, and yet, it never feels chaotic. Her control and restraint are excellent, and she's clearly a writer to watch–and fortunately, you can. Her debut novella *Krackle's Last Movie* launches February 10th.

Vito Gulla holds an MFA in creative writing from Wilkes University and teaches American literature at Thomas Jefferson University. His short fiction has appeared in Pithead Chapel, The Big Click, and Mulberry Fork Review.

The Horoscope Essay
by Nicholas De Marino

Here we are on Starship Earth, ready-set-going lap number four-point-five billion and fifty-two around the Great Yellow Dwarf, poised to mow down each and every hurdle, even though it'd be easier to jump, duck, or run around the damned things. Be not grouchy, like so many dwarves barreling up a creek without a pelorus. Whirl and twirl your axes with ecstatic glee like Tasmanian berserkers drunk on TikTok Sufism until the Great Cosmic Nightlights come down from the sky to reveal the secret that we're not alone—just in Cosmic Time Out.

While planetary magnates conspire in constellations, we're left reading tea leaves. That's right, fellow cosmonauts, it's time for a little light-speed, terracentric, astral geometry. I have connected the dots, I have seen the future, and, quite frankly, it's wordy.

Over the lips and past the gums, look out 2026, please no bombs... and ease up on the neocolonial exploitation of Africa.

Aries, the Ram Pickup (March 21-April 19)

The sooner you ditch that New Year's resolution, the better. Let someone else be first to swim the Weddell Sea. In fact, avoid Antarctic travel altogether.

Media Prescription: Rewatch the Key and Peele Wendell skits. The Mr. T PSA, too. If someone really needs the washing machine, they'll throw your clothes on the floor.

Taurus, the Red Buff (April 20-May 20)

Don't be afraid to go off script. Unlike the Betty Boop iconography on her grave marker, Gram-Gram's homemade Four Loko recipe isn't set in stone.

Media Prescription: Binge "Richard Hatem's Paranormal Bookshelf" while DIY-ing crown molding in a last-ditch effort to get back your security deposit.

Gemini, fhe Olsen Twins (May 21-June 20)

Let's face it: No one wants to hear your retro swing band's original material. Stick to the classics. Ditto for in the bedroom.

Media Prescription: Ask your therapist if Dan Rath's comedy special, "I'm Not Doing Well Folks," is right for you.

Crab, fhe Cancer (June 21-July 22)

Stop trying to stop trying and just let it happen. You're gonna have to use your whole ass for this one.

Media Prescription: Watch "Elling" for the fifth time this year while palm-to-mouthing popcorn peppered with dry harissa.

Leo, fhe Lion King (July 23-Aug. 22)

You're on the right path. Waze says so. Show the officer. Tell her to save the Korzybski quotes for Tinder and your court appearance.

Media Prescription: Blast SΔMMUS's Pieces in Space on the bus. Everyone will thank you for sharing a decade-old nerdcore classic.

Virgo, fhe No Slut-Shaming Here (Aug. 23-Sept. 22)

Make sure to wash the mint after you've swiped it from the neighbor's garden. Her corgi's been pissing there all week.

Media Prescription: No one wants to read Proust, but it's important—or something.

Libra, the Weight Watchers (Sept. 23-Oct. 22)

The aerial roots on your windowsill succulents mean you're doing something wrong. Avoid tamasic indulgences like Reddit and horoscopes.

Media Prescription: Rewatch the first two seasons of "The Walking Dead." Hey, Shane was actually a pretty good step-dad.

Scorpio, the Strap-on Wielding Harvestman (Oct. 23-Nov. 21)

Say yes more. "A regret" is just an anagram of "greater." Or "get rear."

Media Prescription: Anything but 311's tiki bar-style version of "Lovesong." It was cute for three months in 2004. Give it a rest.

Sagittarius, the Archer Reverse BoJack Horseman Thing (Nov. 22-Dec. 21)

The whole BBL thing is a bubble and, like all bubbles, it's going to burst. Invest now and strike while the booty's bountiful.

Media Prescription: Mohammad-Reza Shajarian. You're welcome.

Ophiuchus, the Freudian Joke (Nov. 29-Dec. 17)

Speak your truth to the world. Your YouTube channel was already on its way to demonetization.

Media Prescription: The eschatology of Joachim of Fiore makes great bedtime reading.

Capricorn, the Little Goat Mermaid (Dec. 22-Jan. 19)

Buy a toner printer to save on legal paperwork-related cartridge costs. Fridge magnets are a cost-effective alternative to a filing cabinet.

Media Prescription: Dorian Feigenbaum's 1933 translation of Victor Tausk's 1919 banger, "On the Origin of the 'Influencing Machine' in Schizophrenia."

Aquarius, the I'm Also an Actor (Jan. 20-Feb. 18)

Avoid dairy products and family members who are still talking about "The Wire." It's never too late to take up competitive ice hockey.

Media Prescription: Sora 2 A.I. knockoffs of those cringy raps from the OG run of G.L.O.W.

Pisces, the Sketchy Sushi Restaurant (Feb. 19-March 20)

This time a wig and a fake name won't be enough. Time for Plan B: I will shift. I will shift. I will shift.

Media Prescription: The animated version of "Room on the Broom" narrated by Simon Pegg.

The Missed Connections Essay
by Nicholas De Marino

"Waste neither Time nor Money, but make the best Use of both."
—that guy on the bills you roll up for coke, you know, Jack Black from the OG Drunk History videos on Funny or Die

I'm in. Yes, seriously! You've been banging on about the One True Faith for twenty-eight minutes and I'm tapping out. Maybe you've never gotten this far. You're like those missionaries in *"Black Books"* who don't know what to do after they're invited in. Look, I can't be the buyer *and* the seller. My usual role is Doubting Thomas, but that ain't feasible across the language barrier. We're finger painting with primary colors here. Also, there's only two minutes left in this English lesson, and I've gotta wrap on a positive note. The five bucks I get for this doesn't mean a thing if you tank my rating and bury me in the algorithm. This used to be my backup gig—grammar note: "used to be" vs. "be used to"— but now it's putting table scraps on the, um, table. Hopefully my missus is as supportive as Olivia Coleman in that *"Bruiser"* sketch where Martin Freeman goes full halal. Hey, what's your stance on orthodoxy vs. orthopraxy? A relevant idiom: pay lip service. That pun's an Easter egg for your A.I. agent when you scrape this class video later.

Immortal souls are boring. Time for some *"Dandy's World."* Yes, a Roblox game. My daughter plays, okay? She loves griefing me, but it's only fun if I'm competent enough to make it past a few floors. This is the most time I've sunk into a game since blowing a hundred hours on *"Final Fantasy*

VII" and still never beating Ruby Weapon or Emerald Weapon. *"Dandy's World"* is a children's survival horror game. The baddies aren't really baddies. Most are just warped versions of playable characters who chase you around an abandoned daycare center. I want to say it's like *"Five Nights at Freddy's,"* but only know that game via an old *"Honest Game Trailer"* I saw when I was all caught up on *"Zero Punctuation"* that week. Anyway, it takes eight hours of gameplay/ exposure therapy to dull the wet thud that rattles your heart each time an antagonist tags you. It sounds like a paper bag of eggs being thumped with a lead pipe.

No, wait, that's an incoming call. God, I hope I don't have to explain passive voice again. Oh, it's you again. Thanks for reading my profile between bookings. At least half of what's there is true. The pirate flag? Well, as my daughter and Pusha-T say, if you know, you know. The rainbow flag? Yeah, I'm fam. "Family." Me? Not really, but I support the community... sure, if you want to get into it, but I don't think... "Furries." As long as we're on a tangent, what animal would you be..? King of the jungle, indeed. Good luck with the harem... okay... I think you mean "gay agenda," but... I'm glad you're aware of "cultural relativity," but that goes both ways, lil' homie... okay, okay, that's enough. Your grammar's fine. Some relevant vocab: false equivalency, argument from authority, and inalienable rights. Also "passive-aggressive," which is what I'm being right now. Feel free to drone on as I open another tab and feel mildly ashamed clicking the "I'm an adult" pop-up on *Fandom*'s Dandy's World Wiki.

Drip. Drip. Drip. The goal of each level is to pause your game of hide and seek with the baddies to steal their oil. Sorry, "ichor," which, apparently I've been mispronouncing with an "ick" for four decades. The black viscous substance of power collects in giant containers with Eye-of-Sauron-like indicator lights and makes a piddling noise that reminds you exactly how many cups of coffee, black tea, and yerba mate you've drank—no, drunk. There are also occasional toxic leaks and blackouts. (Jesus, I miss drinking.) The corrupted bad guys are covered in this Oil-It's-Not stuff, and it makes them red-eyed and cray-cray. Oh yeah, and if you don't buy things from the in-game store with the in-game currency, the titular rainbow-colored flower/war profiteer goes apeshit. Speaking of blowhards, that student's still blathering...

"Escort." Register in English is tricky for natives, let alone ESL speakers. That's doubly true when it comes to fucking and, from what you're describing, Moroccan sex tourism, exploitation and, quite possibly, human trafficking. You balked at "prostitute," but I, sir, balk at your use of "bitch." You know, I get a lot of adults who use English lessons as discount therapy and confessionals, but I detect neither shame nor regret in your voice. Usage: "Either, or" vs. "neither, nor." On the other hand, you're too clumsy to be one of those NLP/*"The Game"* pickup artists. Maybe those girls are better off placating your ego an extra day as a "freebie" than being abused by pimps or crueler johns.

Le sigh. All of this makes me sad.

But, back in *"Dandy's World,"* the kids are working together, adopting *Mission Impossible*-style roles as "extractors" and "distractors," and siphoning resources from the failed sigil-branded institutions of yesteryear. They're redistributing tools, meme-ing in nearly incomprehensible hat-on-hat language, and shipping characters who profess a spectrum of pronouns. They might rat out jerks in chat, but they also grief each other for lulz. Maybe this next generation will do better. Maybe the kids are al—

WHY DID YOU LITTLE ASSHOLES VOTE FOR DYLE'S FLOOR WHEN I ONLY HAVE ONE HEART?

Never mind, we're fucked. See you next round. Inshallah.

Nicholas De Marino needs a hug. Poetry in Dreams & Nightmares and Horrific Scribblings. Fiction in BULL and Hell Itself. Monthly columns (fnord) in foofaraw and The Independent Variable. ¡Viva SFPA y Codex! No awards but some nominations.

More at nicholasdemarino.blogspot.com.

Interview with Ashlee Lhamon

Do you "bring your whole self to work"? Should people?

Well, now that I'm writing full time, definitely yes–I think writing is easiest when you've got some real life experience to base it on. Back when I worked in an office? God no. Honestly, it seems like a weird idea to me. I don't know any of these people! Knowing more about them just makes me like them less! Maybe if you were working at a cool startup where you'd just hired all of your college friends, but how many of us get to do that?

Also, it's totally a fake intimacy ploy to try and get you to work longer hours for less money. Just saying.

Why the vendetta against HR?

With some rare exceptions, Human Resources exists to protect the company from getting sued. They will totally screw you over if it's in the company's best interests.

Our protagonist seems a tad bit self-absorbed; are they based on someone you know or dare I ask, is there a little bit of yourself in them?

So, this story is more of a satire on the trope that follows a very traditionally lit, navel-gazey character with traditionally lit interpersonal problems through a science fiction and fantasy plot or setting. Like, "My husband and I were getting a divorce but now he's turned into a werewolf and his flesh-hungry tearing through the local school board is complicating my feelings about our relationship" or "This alien invasion is really highlighting my dissatisfaction with my associate creative writing professorship at this small liberal arts college." In my personal internal TVTropes I call them Moon Dramas, which is where the tongue-in-cheek title of this story comes from.

But also, you definitely have to be self-absorbed to write satire, so yes, probably this character is me.

Are these early moon settlers or is there an established society up there?

Ooh, great question! I would probably say early settlers because it feels like they would have already awoken the horrible moon creatures with a large civilization. On the other hand, they have brought HR up, which feels like big civilization stuff . . . hmm . . . I would love to say I know every aspect of every story I write but uh . . .

Given the protagonist's aloofness, do you think they end up having the same fate as their co-workers or do they survive and live to see another work day or even make it back down to Earth?

Oh they definitely get eaten. Their final thoughts are that this is also a metaphor.

How many times has this story been rejected from other mags?

Foofaraw is actually the first place I sent it! It's been hanging out on my laptop for a while, waiting for the perfect market, and Foofaraw seemed like home.

What's a great short story you've read recently?

I've been reading the newest Radon Journal and while it's hard to pick a favorite, I think "Killing Yourself" by Evan Simon-Leack is my favorite so far! I love pulp, and it's such a great pulpy noir with a real emotional punch. (Also, clones. I'm really into clones right now).

Do you have anything else you'd like to share?

Shameless self-promotion time: I'm in the latest issue of Apex Magazine with my flash piece, *Shrinkage!* and my clifi solarpunk story *Sandbag Squidward* is going to be featured with Grist's Imagine 2200.

But otherwise, check out Dream Theory Media! Friends and fellow writers M.M. Schrier and Jacob Baugher are sharing an issue there, and they are simply amazing!

Interview with Rachel Davey

Have you ever been robbed?

Yes, I have. This story was actually based on last summer when my phone was stolen from me, my glasses broke, my laptop was spilled on (and broke) and then a ton of my clothes were stolen out of my moving van. All of this happened in rapid succession, and by the end, I felt kind of resigned to it.

Does the protagonist ever get back to living a "normal" life with things and without a personal thief?

I don't know. To me, the protagonist's story ends where the actual story does. I literally feel like I can't even imagine what she'd do next. I suppose she functions as more of an exploration of a certain facet of myself than a real person.

If you knew someone broke into your house, do you think you'd try to confront them or lay perfectly still?

I would definitely try to confront them. Honestly, if they weren't threatening me, I might let them take a few things.

Do you suffer from being too much of a people pleaser?

I can! I am trying to be better about it, and I suppose that's what this story is somewhat about. Aside from all my stuff getting stolen, the story's inspiration came from a conversation with a friend about how we hoped the thieves needed my stuff more than I did, and it made me curious about the point at which giving becomes giving your entire self away.

How many times has this story been rejected by other markets?

I don't know the exact amount, but it has been rejected. So has all of my other work that's eventually been published. It just goes to show that taste is subjective. Also, in this field everyone has to be rejected sometimes, so when it happens to me, it's a check off the list. I just think about how I'm that much closer to being accepted!

What's a great short story you've read recently?

"A Manual for Cleaning Women" by Lucia Berlin! It also mentions stealing.

What book are you reading right now?

The Blood of Others by Simone de Beauvoir

Do you have anything else you'd like to share?

You can read my other work <u>here</u>, <u>here</u> or <u>here</u>. Thank you!

Interview with B. Morris Allen

The first thing people tend to think of these days when they see the word "algorithm" is typically tech related—that's not the case with this story. Was that dissonance intentional?

I recognized the dissonance, but I can't say it was really intentional. I stole the phrase "Escape Algorithm" from Fran Wilde during a discussion 15 years ago. I think we were either both going to use it as a prompt or write something together; I don't recall, and nothing ever came of it. It's been slowly simmering in the back of my mind since then, until, quite recently it re-emerged as this story. I'd been failing to write a tech story based off the idea when it came to me that 'algorithm' didn't really *have* to be tech related, and then this flowed quite easily.

The protagonist of the story seems meticulous in the way she numbers every page and wants to get everything just right. Is that just her nature, or is it a lesson learned from over 3,000 days in captivity and a strong desire to get out?

I see that as simply her nature; she's tenacious and methodical. But she definitely has also learned from her failure.

Do you think you'd have the willpower to keep at it after 3,000 days of meticulousness and failure?

I can be methodical and tenacious when I decide something needs to be done. However, my first attempts tend to be much more instinctive - trying the things that *feel* right. In this protagonist's situation, I frankly doubt I'd be able to maintain the anger and bitterness; I'd probably just get down to making the best of it after a while.

Do you think she gets her revenge?

I think she does, or at least keeps trying. She's one of those people who just never forgets a slight. I don't think she'd ever be able to let it go.

If you were to escape something like this, do you think you'd immediately start planning your revenge or would you try to get as far away as possible from the people who did this to you?

I can be as petty as the next person, and I do react strongly to what I see as injustice. However, I also hope I'd see that if the only injustice was to me, there would be better things to do with my life than exact vengeance.

Does this idea of needing to be exact in creating this recipe/spell come from your former career of being a biochemist?

I think that her meticulous notes probably do link back somewhere to the lab notebooks we all kept - what we planned, what actually occurred, what the result was. If you really want to learn from experimentation, good records are essential.

How many times has this story been rejected from other mags?

According to Submission Grinder, it was rejected exactly 10 times.

What's a great short story you've read recently?

I read a collection (*When Mothers Dream*) by Brenda Cooper, whom I'd known very little of, and really liked the story "Southern Residents", about a young influencer exposed to the work of a marine conservatory.

What book are you reading right now?

I've always got a few books going. Right now, they include *Mercury Rising* by R.W.W. Greene, *Mud and Brass* by Andrew Knighton, and some NetGalley selections, *The Castle and the Cloister* by Laura E. Weymouth and *Not With a Bang* by Temi Oh.

Do you have anything else you'd like to share?

Speaking of rejection, I'm in the final stages of editing *TRUNK: stories that took the long way*, which is an anthology of original SFF stories that were rejected many times - anywhere from 11 (for a novelette) to almost 50 (for a short story). Submitting stories can be incredibly tedious, but publishing is a question of finding the right editor for the right story, and it's one circumstance where tenacity really can pay off. I'm aiming to have the anthology out around mid-year - keep your eyes open for it!

Interview with Monica Louzon and Isis Aquino

Monica Louzon

What was it about this story that made you want to translate it?

There are several different kinds of poignant loneliness in this story that resonated with me, and I'm a sucker for literally star-crossed lovers.

Are you much of a stargazer?

Yes! I don't have my own telescope, but I grew up peering through my dad's telescope on cold winter nights at the Moon, Jupiter, and rings of Saturn (other stuff, too, I'm sure, but those three made the biggest impression on me). Nowadays, I'm always looking up at night - you can often find me walking my dog in the dark, letting him lead me while I stare up at the stars and try to spot the ISS.

Who do you see yourself in more, Lenny or Skylar?

Lenny. There's a point in the story where Lenny tries to come up with a way to give Skylar hope, but can't think of anything, so he instead tries to distract her by talking about random things that come to mind - I can relate so hard to this conundrum, and and absolutely employ this exact same strategy in similar situations. (I have lots of trains of thought going at any one time, which makes it easy to distract people with them!)

How many times has this story been rejected?

It took 54 submissions over 3.5 years before foofaraw accepted this translation. We got 12 personal rejections and 2 holds in the process (which didn't overlap, interestingly enough)!

What book are you reading right now?

I don't often read nonfiction, but I am thoroughly enjoying Terry Pratchett: A Life With Footnotes: The Official Biography (2022) by Rob Wilkins. Rob was Terry's personal assistant and heavily pulled upon Terry's own notes toward his incomplete memoir/autobiography to finish this biography for Terry.

Do you have anything else you'd like to share?

If you want to read about librarian drama and books that make pearls (like oysters!), check out (ha!) my story "Shorthand" over at After the Storm Magazine - it came out in January 2026!

I'm really excited to have 3 more translations for different authors coming out during the first half of 2026:

1. "Letters From a Dead Girl" by Santiago Eximeno, which is a horror microfiction forthcoming in Dreams & Nightmares Magazine,

2. "The Sea's Decree" by Armando Boix, which is a folk horror/dark fantasy novelette coming out in Adventures BookZine, and

"Above the Sand, Under the Skin" by Ramiro Sanchiz, which is a weird science fiction story forthcoming from Translunar Travelers Lounge.

*

Isis Aquino

When you think about what could be out beyond this galaxy, do you get hopeful or pessimistic?

Definitely hopeful. I'm not sure we will ever have the technology to travel through space at super high speeds or do anything depicted in space operas, but I'm absolutely positive that we'll be discovering new phenomena and understanding more about the universe and the way it works.

Despite being in a terrible position, there is a gracefulness in the way Skylar handles herself. Do you think you'd have the same grace in that situation, at that age?

No way! I would be a mess! But as my father used to say, each generation of children tends to be more aware of itself and the reality around them at earlier ages. I guess that I was trying to depict a teenager that is composed and calm as a result of this tendency towards precocity as a result of an overall advancement in future societies.

Who do you see yourself in more, Lenny or Skylar?

I'd say Lenny, because he's a smart kid but also kinda awkward. I tend to feel awkward even if I'm really not.

What's a great short story you've read recently?

"Mouthful of birds" by Samantha Schweblin. I found it unsettling in an enjoyable way.

What book are you reading right now?

It's in Spanish, it's an anthology of science fiction written by Puerto Rican women. Its title is "Distopía nuestra de cada día" with a go word by Puerto Rican scholar Angela M. Valentin Rodriguez. All the short stories are mind blowing!

Do you have anything else you'd like to share?

There is a short story I read a couple years ago that stuck with me, it was written by Monica Louzon who happens to have translated my stories into English. The title is "Mother's Love" and I think about it almost every month. Any woman who reads it will know why.

Interview with H. Marin

There's a wonderful contrast between beautiful prose and a quite dark and ugly situation... was that deliberate or just natural from your writing style and interests?

I find this question to be incredibly satisfying because it's a question I've gotten pretty much my whole life (looking at you, Mr. Turtola from high school Creative Writing), so I have to imagine that it's an intrinsic part of my writing style. I personally love the juxtaposition between beautiful words and horrifying concepts.

Trauma seems to be a major theme in this story; do you sometimes view writing as a way to work through your own trauma and/or problems?

Oh, absolutely. Trauma informs pretty much all of my work. Some of my pieces have main characters who persevere despite seemingly insurmountable odds, but some are sucked into disastrous situations far beyond their understanding; darkness becomes a normalized part of life. Even in this way, though, I try to impart the understanding that living with darkness is normal. Beauty can be found even in the darkest places. Acceptance, in and of itself, is healing.

I know it's a bit cliché to ask where a story comes from, but does this come from a more personal place or is it more a reflection of the monstrous times we seem to be living in?

At the heart of this story is Val's desire to be a good parent despite all the wrongs she has suffered in her life and, as a result, she has inadvertently inflicted on her child. That being said, I absolutely think that I address an issue very personal to me. I know I'm not alone in the occasional thought that I am not doing right by my children, even if I'm doing the best I can with what I have. Val represents perseverance; the ability to keep going when we feel like we can't bear the cards we've been dealt.

Do you view the ending as hopeful or do you think Valeria is likely to struggle getting her life on track?

I think Val turning down the endless possibility only a god can offer is absolutely a turning point for her. It's my belief that as soon as she sees her daughter again, she's going to have a reason to turn it all around, which is a purpose I think she was lacking when she met Iggy. This story is, unfortunately, based on grim realities—the girls who fall through the cracks and think they can do no better, the people who are queued up to take advantage. I want Val to act as a shining beacon of hope in an otherwise desolate landscape. It's never too late.

Do you have any experience with house-sitting? Any strange or memorable moments?

Funnily enough I have never house-sat, although I am that person who is afraid of the dark and practically runs up basement stairs. I genuinely think a lot of this story came from my general distaste of basements and/or attics.

How many times has this story been rejected by other markets?

This piece had 14 rejections before it found its home. A lot of the time it truly is a matter of finding the right editor for a piece!

What's a great short story you've read recently?

I'm currently working my way through Cosmic Horror Monthly's *Aseptic and Faintly Sadistic: An Anthology of Hysteria Fiction*, and I really enjoyed Kelsea Yu's "China Doll". I think it also touches on a lot of similar themes from Basement Girls.

What book are you reading right now?

I am reading Oscar Wilde's *The Portrait of Dorian Gray*.

Interview with A.J. Hodges

Are you a pub or a club kind of person?

100% club! Or a small live punk concert. The older I am, the more I get the appeal of a pub with a cozy fireplace, though.

What's your experience/opinion of EDM?

If it gets people dancing in a good way, I'm all for it. I loved minimal techno and electroclash back in the day (was low-key shocked to learn this is now a retro thing).

Best experience: Seeing Autechre play at Berghain in Berlin. But is that EDM or IDM?

Do you have any Lucys in your life? Past or present?

Past—definitely! This story was partly addressed to my teenage self, after all.

Present—thankfully not. Maybe if I was still working in academia, I encountered a few there...

We often think about the arts and creativity as things that make the world a better place so there is something a bit subversive about flipping that on it's head and stealing the creativity of the youth

to make the city a better place; was this intentional or more of an afterthought?

I've been thinking a lot about the extractive aspect to many (not all) social media platforms recently (shout-out to <u>Off the Grid</u>), and how the feed can lull us into a hypnotic state, while profiting off other people's creativity—the influencer slash content creator model. I think that's what inspired me, but it wasn't a conscious decision at the time of writing. There are no smartphones in the story.

If you wanted to put someone into a musically induced trance/coma, what music do you think you'd play?

Easy question! Boards of Canada. One of my favorite bands. Maybe "1969" or "Buckie High"?

How many times has this story been rejected by other markets?

This story has been rejected twice by other markets. And I submitted an older version to a music-themed short-story competition that I didn't win, obv.

What's a great short story you've read recently?

I keep returning to "The Longest Season in the Garden of the Tea-Fish."

What book are you reading right now?

I always have a few books on the go! Right now it's *Deep Wheel Orcadia* (Harry Josephine Giles), *Red, White, and Royal*

Blue (Casey McQuiston), and *Gathering Moss* (Robin Wall Kimmerer)

Do you have anything else you'd like to share?

I used to live in Croatia and Serbia, and I've been collaborating with some awesome writers from there. I recently had this literary horror translation published on the *Asymptote Journal* blog. And a big shout-out to my friends at Shtriga Books – Croatia's one and only queer speculative fiction press.

Interview with Tyler Lee

Given it's a ghost train, I'm dying to know if the paint will still be there when the train returns the next week...

That's a great question! I hope so, but even as the writer of the story, I can't tell you that for sure. I think one of the things that's really special about graffiti (whether ghost-infused or not) is that it's ephemeral and unpredictable. You could throw a tag on a wall Friday night and it might be painted over by Monday afternoon, or it might still be there a decade later. I think some of this comes across in the story (I hope) but one of the things I love about graffiti is that it's an art where so much of the value seems to be in the *doing* – in the process of creation itself – rather than in the outcome of that production. It's not really about making something that you can hold in your hand forever.

You know there's a shelf-life, but you don't often know exactly how long that will be. When you think about trains, too, even if a train comes by every week, the cars attached to that train could be totally different ones. I live a few blocks away from a train yard and sometimes I'll see them switching cars out and I wonder where that specific car is going, where it's been before. You never know for sure.

What's your own experience with street art, if any?

As a teenager I would say I "dabbled" with graffiti, but I want to make it very clear that I was never even the slightest bit actually *good* at it. Back alley stuff either out with a friend or, more often, alone on my bike, basically. Sharpie tags mostly, or else a friend would find some cheap hardware store spray-paint in his uncle's shed or something like that, and we'd paint dumb stuff on the back wall of the corner store or some person's garage door. Typical bored delinquent kid stuff, really. I think I *wanted* to be good at it, but I've never had a knack for that sort of fine motor control. Even my regular handwriting is atrocious. I stopped that when I reached the level of awareness needed to be embarrassed by my output, haha.

Then, when I was more in my 20s, I started doing this thing where I'd carry around Sharpies and label paper in my backpack everywhere, and then when I was sitting on the bus or whatever, or really whenever an idea hit me, I'd take out the label paper and write short, immediate poems on them. A few lines, or a few words, or an image or idea that hit me. Every now and then, I'd cut all the ones I'd written recently out, and then wander around town sticking them up on things. I don't think many of them survived the weather all that long, but I like to think at least a few people saw them and thought about them for a second or two.

But being part of the hip-hop community, I'm always around graffiti. I see my homies flipping through their blackbooks, see pieces they benched on their IG feeds, hear them talk about stuff. There's an incredible festival in Saskatoon (my hometown) called Summer Fling, where artists from all over the world come into town to do pieces. I go hang out every year, listen to music, talk to people, and watch them paint.

So I guess the tl-dr version of this essay is, I have *a little* experience, but I also feel like I have an amount of distance from it to where graff still feels like some kind of impossible magic to me. I think a lot of that comes through in the story.

How does your music, fiction, and street art overlap and/or compare & contrast against each other?

Hip-hop is really a story-telling genre at its core. I'm basically baby-deer fresh to writing prose fiction, but I think some of those story-telling instincts have followed me over from the song-writing. I'd say the biggest difference between the two (in terms of my approach, personally) is that the audience for a short story arrives expecting fiction, and all that entails – some kind of narrator, some kind of point-of-view, the possibility of fantastical things happening. In a hip-hop song I think the audience's default assumption is usually that the material will be realistic and at least semi-autobiographical, so you have to do a little bit of table-setting to create that distinction between "me" the writer of the song, and "me" the narrator of the song if you are going to do something outright fictional. Most of my prose writing is "weird" in one way or another – there's some kind of fantastical, speculative, or surreal element, or just an absurd energy to them – whereas my instinct with song-writing is almost always to play things relatively straight and earnest.

Another thing that I think connects both of these artistic practices (along with poetry/spoken word, which I also dabble in) is just the musicality of words. I love really satisfying phonetics, rhythmic, flowing sentences, alliteration, rhyme – all that good stuff – and while those sorts of devices are certainly more prominent in the music and the poetry, I try to imbue a bit of that musical energy into my prose, too. Still very much a work in progress, but a skill that I'm trying to nurture and develop right now.

You mentioned to me you originaſſy wrote this for a cſass—was there a prompt or fheme or device you were taſked wifh utilizing? If so, what was fhe fhrough-line fhat led you to fhis ſtory?

There was no particular prompt or instruction for this assignment, beyond writing a complete story. For myself, I'd set a bit of a personal goal of blending the magical with the local. I feel like Saskatchewan is not a place that most people know much about, or think about very often, but I've lived almost my entire life here. It can be a deceptively strange place beneath the surface. I wrote four pieces in fairly quick succession that are all sort of dream-like ruminations on the history, politics, identity, and landscape (both physical and psychological) of this place. "Good Bones" was published with Neon & Smoke recently. Another will be published in Spring Magazine (which is a publication local to Saskatchewan, run by the Saskatchewan Writer's Guild) in April, while the last (my favourite of the four, actually) is still out on submission.

If I'm not miſtaken, fhis wiſſ be your fhird publiſhed ſtory, foſſowing "Good Bones" at Neon & Smoke, and "Memory Revisions" at Radon Journal... what has your experience been getting ſtarted in fhis world and what litmags were you reading fhat eventuaſſy led you

to try your hand at writing and submitting?

To give the readers a bit of context, as I'm typing it's just past midnight, February 5th. My Neon & Smoke publication came out on January 21st, while the Radon Journal issue launched on February 1st, so this is all very *very* new to me. I will admit when I first started submitting things I was only really familiar with a few litmags, all of which are Canadian, aside from like The New Yorker. Grain Magazine is a journal that's local to Saskatchewan, but is well-known in CanLit circles, and I've been reading it off-and-on since high school after a favourite teacher introduced me to it. Augur is another Canadian magazine that I love.

Basically the story is this: I was downsized from my long-time job during the pandemic and decided to go to online school and get an undergraduate degree in English. After a couple of semesters of introductory courses, I was able to start taking creative writing classes. I kind of figured I was a "good" writer, but I thought I was like "good" for someone who isn't *really* a writer, if that makes any sense. Like, you could be cracking the hell out of the ball in the batting cages after work, and having a lot of fun doing it, but that doesn't mean you belong at the plate against even a single-A level pitcher. I kind of figured that was what I was – pretty good for the batting cages, but please keep him off the diamond. It was one of my creative writing professors who really encouraged me to start submitting my pieces for publication, though. At first I was very hesitant and reserved – I made just a few submissions here and there, assumed nothing would come from it, but still got disheartened at the rejections anyway haha. But then I got a few almost-successes. A hold here, a personal rejection there. Enough to keep me going at least, if only at the snail's pace I was comfortable with at the time.

The acceptances from Neon & Smoke and Radon Journal happened in very quick succession – I think there might have been less than a week pass between the two emails. Neon & Smoke hadn't published anything yet when I submitted to them, and I think I found them through an algorithmic advertisement on Instagram. Radon I discovered because I was specifically looking for anarchist-leaning spec fic to read, and they popped up in my search.

The Radon acceptance was a game-changer, though, because (as you know, but maybe the readers don't) Radon runs an incredible Discord server. I've learned so much just through seeing the conversations the veterans are having – interesting markets, tools to use, submission strategies, all sorts of things. There's also just a level of irreverence and camaraderie that helped melt away a lot of my rejection anxiety and has made me a lot more willing to yeet stuff out and see what happens. I discovered foofaraw through the Radon Discord, too, and you've fast become one of my favourite outlets to read.

It feels like Jake reaches some catharsis through tagging the ghost train and going from "HERE" to "GONE" and not needing the a copy of the photos, but externally, not much has changed… Am I reading too much into this or is this cathartic feeling intentional, and if so, what do you think it is about this specific tag that achieves this?

Yes, very much intentional. I hope my explanation won't be too scrambled here, but I'm going to do my best to share my perspective. In the Canadian national myth, trains played a massive role as a connecting-force, bridging the gap between the populous, "cultured" Eastern provinces, and the "frontier" in the West. Obviously, the real history of Western expansion is much more complicated (and much darker) than that, but this is what most of us are taught as children, and I think that idea remains part of the public imagination. But just as settlements built up quickly around these rail-lines, they died out just as fast when rail stopped being as important. In a sense, Chapel Head is an outpost whose connection to the outside world has been severed, aside from this brief, flashing moment on this one little stretch of decommissioned track.

I think one thing about Jake is that he (like a lot of kids in small towns, especially kids who don't conform as well to the environment) feels fundamentally trapped in Chapel Head. The notion of being stuck in place is a big theme of the story, with all of the other ghosts (aside from the train) being essentially defined by the places they haunt. Jake's also a little bit invisible – his father is usually absent, and when he's around he's abusive. Jake doesn't have a large friend group or any real social circle beyond Gabe. That's kind of what his "HERE" tags really represent – it's almost like a prisoner scratching his name in the wall of his cell, "Jake was here" – both as an observation of the place that he's stuck in, but also just an assertion that he's a being who exists in the world, in this dark corner that no one is looking at. I think maybe more than any character I've ever written, there's a LOT of myself in Jake. He's very sensitive – he feels deeply – but he's also introverted, reserved, hesitant to take up more space in the world than he feels he deserves, yet also chafing at the discomfort of that tiny box that he's put himself in. The feelings and thoughts inside of him wind up bleeding out through his tags, because he doesn't give them any other avenue to be expressed.

Over the course of the story, though, his perspective shifts in some small but meaningful ways. Theron is a new person in Jake's life but he does small things that make Jake feel seen. Firstly, Jake initially thinks that painting the train is impossible, Theron doesn't just think it's possible, but he thinks *Jake* should be part of doing it. Theron sticks up for Jake when he's being bullied in the cafeteria. Jake "slips" (in his own eyes) when he hints at his father's abuse in front of Theron in the woods – he exposes something about himself that he prefers to keep hidden – but Theron neither pushes the issue, nor ridicules him, instead Theron offers him comfort. At the same time, Jake gets to see Chapel Head a little bit through Theron's eyes and become reacquainted with some of the magic and the beauty of the prairies that Jake had become a little bit blind to, which influences the way he paints his GONE tag, in all the sunset colours and soft, ambiguous shapes.

The other thing is that the ghost train is going to be leaving. It's going out into the world – away from Chapel Head. The prisoner might scratch "Jake was here" into his cell wall, but that's not the sort of message he would write on a letter that he planned to throw over the wall in the hopes someone else might find it – I don't think that letter would say where the person is, I think they'd want to say who they are. I guess the GONE tag is kind of like that. It's about Jake coming to recognize something inherently beautiful (or at least valuable) inside himself that he had been blind to, doing his best to turn that beauty into shapes and colours, and then sending it out, hoping that someone sees it. He doesn't need a picture of the finished piece, because painting it was the important part. He writes GONE because the piece is going to be gone as soon as he's finished painting it, and he's okay with that.

But also, the story starts with Jake being asked to do a thing, and him saying that it's impossible to do. The story ends with Jake doing that impossible thing. I think that's a really transformative experience for anyone, not just to do a thing that's difficult, or even to do a thing that other people told you that you couldn't do, but to do a thing that you told *yourself* you couldn't do. I think the final moments of the story, with Jake in his bedroom listening to *Aquemini* and thinking about a train just starting to pick up speed from a dead stop sort of represent the first time in Jake's life where he's realizing that he might have been wrong about himself. That he's not so much trapped as he is just stopped, and that if he wants to start moving forward, he can. It won't happen immediately, it won't happen without effort, but it will happen, so long as he chooses to.

How many times has this story been rejected?

I think this one has only been rejected once. I wrote it for a creative writing class, and I liked it a lot personally (as did my professor) but I wasn't sure if it was really relevant to the broader public. Part of that is just my own insecurity, but I also worried that people who didn't know much about Saskatchewan, and that people who didn't know much about graffiti, would both find it kind of esoteric and alienating. But then, after seeing a bunch of people on the Radon Journal Discord championing the "when in doubt, yeet it out" mantra, I took the plunge and I'm glad I did.

What's a great short story you've read recently?

The New Yorker released a massive anthology in 2025 commemorating a century of publishing short fiction in their magazine, and I've been surfing through that on my eReader periodically, picking and choosing pieces just based on either the writer or the title. The story "Playing Metal Gear Solid V: The Phantom Pain" by Jamil Jan Kochai absolutely melted my face off, and not just because I'm a big fan of the game. Incredibly inventive, powerful, and it touches so many different themes.

But also (and I promise I'm not pandering) "Joan's Stone on Loan" by Lyss Buchthal, published recently in foofaraw, has a blend of comical absurdity and emotional honesty that just tickles my brain in the perfect spot. I might never look at a statue the same way again. I've suggested this story to I think a half-dozen people in the week or so since I read it.

What book are you reading right now?

I just finished reading *The End of the Ocean* by Maja Lunde a few hours ago, and it gets a strong recommendation from me. Rich characters, gorgeous prose, important themes, and just a staggeringly beautiful ending.

Do you have anything else you'd like to share?

Check out Radon Journal and Neon & Smoke, they both publish tons of great work, and it's all easily accessible online. I also have pieces scheduled for publication in the near future with Spring Magazine, and Grain Magazine. If you're interested in my music, you can find me on most streaming platforms under the name Skizza, or at https:// skizza306.bandcamp.com. I released a new album in December called "Winter Classic" and I'll have a few more releases between now and the end of the year. I'm pretty bad at social media, but my Instagram is @SkizzaFromSask.

Interview with Michael Allen Rose

Do you view this story as a critique of military (and/or corporate) "brainwashing?"

There are certain themes I come back to again and again in my writing, and one of those is the abuse of power. You can bet that in just about any Michael Allen Rose story, eventually the "big bad guy" will be revealed, at least in part as Religion or Capitalism or the Corporation or the Government. One of those "big ol' capital letter" systems that have bloated to the point where although they may be "run by" people, they no longer consider "people" a central concern. So yes, I think even when I'm being glib and funny in my genre fiction, whether it's horror or sci-fi or bizarro or whatever, there's always a layer of social satire underneath that screaming "don't trust the system, it's there to exploit you." I think history will back me up on this.

Were you a military brat, by chance?

I came from a long line of military folks, but actually I was the one who broke the cycle. I was the first kid on my dad's side of the family to go to college and get a liberal arts degrees rather than dropping out of high school and joining the service. I saw what military service did to my dad, who ended up disabled and retired by the time I was three, and thought "Nope." Growing up just down the road from an Air Force base though, certainly had an influence on me. I was surrounded by military brats all through my school years, and befriended several, so I was peripheral to the military in more than a few ways.

What are your feelings on oatmeal? And if you do like it, I'm curious why that was the food you chose for this specific story?

Sometimes, I'll start a story with a title or a line, instead of a fully formed idea. In this case, it was the non-sequiter: "I'm not very happy about it, but I ate the oatmeal." It's a fun challenge, and I highly recommend it for other writers to try. Then, it sat there in a file all alone for several years, until eventually my brain started to mull over things like "Why is my character upset about eating the oatmeal? What does oatmeal mean to them? Were there raisins?" I worked at a call center for a summer back in high school, and hated it. Combined with my natural disgust for corporations and impersonal capitalist systems, the story slowly formed. For the record, I like oatmeal just fine. Most of my experience with it comes from making it for my girlfriend on the weekend (she likes how I make it. The secret is the milk to oats ratio.) Apple cranberry is my meal of choice.

What's the worst job you've ever had?

I've had a variety of crap jobs. In my teen years, I worked as a housekeeper at a hospital, and at one point actually ended up cleaning the floors of the morgue, armed with only a floor buffer. I distinctly recall the sound of the bubbling machines that, I assume, kept bodies in good condition, while being the only person on that floor of the building. I also worked as a dishwasher at a country club, where even little kids had check books of their own. I worked at a pet store for a bit, where I got to scoop handfuls of liquid puppy poo out of cages filled with ill puppies. But believe it or not, my worst job was for a corporation (which shall not be named) just doing office work. The back-stabbing, the cruelty, the social climbing and politics, the mean spirited exhaustion of people, the byzantine paperwork, and the endless glare of the fluorescent lights slowly killing us? I cried on the way to work sometimes.

Do you think it made you as queasy and felt as soul-sucking as Robert's new gig?

In an ideal world, most people would be able to pursue their passions, find meaningful work, and have enough resources to cover their basic needs no matter their employment status. I would imagine, if people were really honest, and you were able to take a poll of every person in the world that works, the majority would probably be generally unhappy with at least some—if not most—aspects of what they do. Especially those people who have no choice but to work in conscience-crushing, soul-sucking jobs they're forced to pretend to care about. So, yeah, because the world we live in is so very far from ideal, I think most people have this experience at least once in their lives, if not many times. Except maybe billionaires, but... screw billionaires.

The ending is both pretty funny and revelatory—we don't know what this thing is, where it comes from, but if we can harness its power for our benefit while "the people" bear the "costs," we are more than happy to be complicit... I

guess that's a long way to tie this back to the current moment we seem to be living through and ask if that rings true to you as well?

Oh absolutely. It's easy to forget that a lot of genre fiction writers, especially in sci-fi and horror, aren't really writing about the future. They're simply looking at the present and extrapolating what they see, taking it to an extreme, and writing a world that's only a couple of tiny changes away from our own. We are living in a time that's hotly politicized, with every aspect of our lives being scrutinized, criticized, and used as fuel for straw-men created by those who don't agree with us so they can justify harm. But even with that tension, most people are happy to sit behind their keyboard, spread conjecture and insults, and not actually seek out verified information or build connections. Or worse yet, listen to "an authority" that definitely doesn't care about them or have any of their interests at heart. They are, as you say, complicit in their own subjugation. Most people don't like to consider consequences, or think long-term. It's inconvenient and unpleasant.

How many times has this story been rejected?

I think the story was rejected around 6 to 8 times from various publications? Interestingly, the first time it got somewhere was in 2024 when it was picked up as a translation for an anthology released by South America's Vestigio Press called *Brecha II: Antología de Literatura ExtraÑa*. It was my first foreign language publication. I wish I could read it, but sadly my public school education failed me, and I can't read Spanish well enough to enjoy it! It was "kept for further consideration" once or twice, but until now, has not seen publication in English. I'm happy that Foofaraw enjoyed it enough to unleash it on the masses!

What's a great short story you've read recently?

This is cheating a little bit, because it's a story in one of the anthologies my own small press RoShamBo Publishing put out, but John Bruni wrote a wonderful story called *Family Tradition* for our *Stories From The Motel Sick* anthology. A man checks into our metaphysical motel to commit suicide, and ends up having a long, dark night of the soul in which he meets the ghosts of his father and his past and breaks a long cycle of violence and mental illness. It's hard to explain further without spoiling it, but for me publishing it was a no-brainer.

What book are you reading right now?

I'm currently in the middle of a true crime book about the murder of Emmett Till called *The Barn: The Secret History of a Murder in Mississippi* by Wright Thompson. It's pretty intense, as you'd imagine. And I just finished an amazing book called *Mother-Eating* by Jess Hagemann that's a horror-tinged retelling of the story of Marie Antionette's reign through the lens of a woman who sells her daughter to a Texas death cult for fame and fortune. In lighter moments, I've been absolutely obsessed with Matt Dinniman's *Dungeon Crawler Carl* series!

Do you have anything else you'd like to share?

I have a Patreon where I release a new zine or chapbook just about every month, so if people like weird, limited edition, hand-mailed stories, plays, and other oddities, that's a good place to get more of me! You can find that, and all sorts of other things at my link tree: <u>http://linktr.ee/</u> <u>michaelallenrose</u>

Also, Bizarro Con is coming up, which is something I've been involved with for years, and is the place I met many of my best friends in writing. Portland, Oregon, May 14-16 2026! If you're a weirdo and haven't found a place your imagination fits in yet, you should check it out. <u>www.bizarrocon.com</u>

Be kind to each other. Please. Help each other out. A rising tide raises all ships.

is...

/ˈfo͞ofəˌrô/
noun:

1. *a great deal of fuss or attention given to a minor matter;*
2. *showy frills added unnecessarily;*
3. *a zine and indie publisher of surreal storytelling and worldly observations.*

Masthead

Kevin Kortum, *Chief exaggeration officer*

Tony Tran, *Director of superfluous beauty*

Jeff Goldberg, *Editor-at-ease*

Megan Diedericks, *Social chronicler of minor disturbances*

and as always
be kind, stay sane